THE
COCKATRICE
BOYS

BOOKS BY JOAN AIKEN

The Haunting of Lamb House
Morningquest
Jane Fairfax
Blackground
If I Were You
Mansfield Revisited
Foul Matter
The Girl from Paris
The Weeping Ash
The Smile of the Stranger
Castle Barebane
Emma Watson

The Five-Minute Marriage
Last Movement
The Silence of Herondale
Voices in an Empty House
A Cluster of Separate Sparks
The Embroidered Sunset
The Crystal Crow
Dark Interval
Beware of the Bouquet
The Fortune Hunters
Eliza's Daughter

JUVENILES

A Creepy Company
A Fit of Shivers
Return to Harken House
Give Yourself a Fright
A Touch of Chill
The Shadow Guests
Midnight Is a Place
A Whisper in the Night
The Wolves of Willoughby Chase
Black Hearts in Battersea
Nightbirds on Nantucket
The Cuckoo Tree
The Stolen Lake
Dido and Pa
Is Underground
The Skin Spinners: Poems
The Green Flash and Other Tales
*The Far Forests: Tales of
    Romance, Fantasy and Suspense*
The Angel Inn by the Comtesse de
    Ségur, translated by Joan Aiken

Bridle the Wind
Go Saddle the Sea
The Teeth of the Gale
The Faithless Lollybird
Not What You Expected
Arabel's Raven
Arabel and Mortimer
*The Mooncusser's Daughter: A
    Play for Children*
Winterthing: A Children's Play
Street: A Play for Children
Died on a Rainy Sunday
Night Fall
*Smoke from Cromwell's Time
    and Other Stories*
The Whispering Mountain
A Necklace of Raindrops
*Armitage, Armitage, Fly Away
    Home*
The Moon's Revenge
Cold Shoulder Road

THE COCKATRICE BOYS

JOAN AIKEN

TOR®

A Tom Doherty Associates Book
New York

THE COCKATRICE BOYS

Copyright © 1993, 1996 by Joan Aiken Enterprises, Ltd.

Interior illustrations by Jason Van Hollander

A Tor Book
Published by Tom Doherty Associates, Inc.
175 Fifth Avenue
New York, NY 10010

Tor Books on the World Wide Web:
http://www.tor.com

Tor® is a registered trademark of Tom Doherty Associates, Inc.

Edited by David G. Hartwell

Library of Congress Cataloging-in-Publication Data

Aiken, Joan.
    The Cockatrice boys / by Joan Aiken. —1st ed.
        p.   cm.
    "A Tom Doherty Associates book."
    ISBN 0–312–86056–0 (acid-free paper)
    I. Title.
PR6051.I35C63   1996
823'.914—dc20   96–8298
                                                          CIP

First Edition: September 1996

Printed in the United States of America

0 9 8 7 6 5 4 3 2 1

To Charles Schlessiger

THE
COCKATRICE
BOYS

Chapter one

Nobody seemed to know where the dreadful things came from. Some people said one thing, some said another.

But experts mostly agree as to the day when the evil invasion of the British Isles first began.

It was on a wretched rainy Sunday in the month of September. Recently the winters had all been bitterly cold and snowy, while the summers were shorter and windier and wetter. On this September Sunday people were coming home from their holidays, flying in from Sardinia and Spain and Sicily. For most of them, wherever they had been, the weather was so nasty that they hardly felt they had been away.

Tired, disgruntled passengers disembarked from their planes at the big airport outside Manchester. They scurried through streaming rain to the airport building, then filed slowly through Passport Control, and began waiting in the baggage claim hall for their luggage to arrive. Soon they hoped to see it come sliding up a moving ramp, tip over the top, and come slithering down on to a travelling circular platform. All the passengers squeezed as close to this platform as possible, hoping to be the first to grab their own bags and hurry off to customs.

But a whole lot of time passed by. People waited and waited. They grumbled more and more loudly as they gazed at the luggage belt, which kept sliding by with nothing on it.

"Only twenty metres walk from our plane," said one woman. "A one-legged rheumatic snail with athlete's foot could have fetched the luggage faster than those handlers are doing it."

"Snails don't have rheumatism," snarled her husband. "And I *told* you, Brenda, only to bring carry-on luggage for a weekend in Brittany."

"It wasn't a weekend, it was five days."

"I can see something coming," said a small pigtailed girl who was with her aunt. She had red hair and looked thin and sad. Oddly enough, from where she stood it wouldn't have been possible to see anything coming up the ramp. But she turned rather pale and her mouth opened in a silent gasp of fright. And then, in a moment, something did come rolling over the summit of the ramp and toppled down the other side.

"*That's* not proper luggage," said the woman called Brenda.

It certainly wasn't. It was an enormously large, lumpy, shapeless sack, tied at the neck with thick rope. It seemed to have some object inside about the size of a sofa but not at all the *shape* of a sofa; this thing, whatever it was, must have had as many corners, dimples, bulges, dents, points, swellings, creases and gibbosities as a seven-ended pineapple. The sack which contained it was uncommonly thick and stout, rather grimy, as if it had travelled half across the world, covered with tags and labels and scribbles, and coloured in wide stripes of orange and purple.

Almost at once it was followed by another sack of a similar kind and quite as large, but a different shape; this one was long, about the length of two beds put end to end, but lumpy, with a fitted bit of the sack covering a kind of prong that stuck up at one end.

"Maybe there's a camel inside it lying down," guessed the pigtailed girl.

"Don't be silly, Sauna," snapped her aunt. "People don't send *camels* in parcels. Oh my stars, I wish our luggage would come. I want to get home. I want my tea."

Everybody wanted to get home and have their tea. Still the luggage did not come. Instead, more and more and more of the large mysterious sacks came trundling up the ramp and tumbling out on to the moving circular beltway, until the whole circle was covered with them, gliding along, one after the other, like a lot of purple and orange ghosts.

"What the *dickens* can they be?" people were saying. "Who do they *belong* to?" "Why doesn't somebody claim them?" "It's not right! There's no room for *our* luggage with all those things out there."

"Maybe they are musical instruments," said the woman called Brenda. "Maybe they belong to one of those pop groups."

"Oh, sure!" snarled her husband, whose name was Ron Glomax. "And what stage in the whole *world* do you think is big enough to hold all those outsize objects? And what do you think they are? Superpianos? Alphorns?"

"Matterhorns, more like," somebody said. "Anyway if they are instruments, where's the group they belong to?"

"P'raps they come from Mars and are stuck at immigration."

"I'm going to complain," said Ron Glomax.

The moving belt was now completely packed with the big shapeless bags, wedged tight as dominoes in a box and all shiny with wet.

"One of them moved!" cried the pigtailed girl.

"Nonsense!" said the aunt. "Stop fidgeting around, Sauna. You stay close by me and behave yourself."

At the end of its track the moving belt travelled through a hole in the wall beyond which was the outside area where the handlers stacked the baggage. This hole was screened by a curtain of swinging leather straps. Beside it was a door marked NO EXIT FOR PASSENGERS. Ron Glomax opened this door and put his head out. But the rain outside was coming down in blinding sheets, so he pulled his head back in again, grumbling that it was all quite disgraceful.

But now, strangely, the number of sacks began to decrease. Gaps appeared between them. Then the gaps became wider. Nobody was seen to take a bag off the belt, yet there were fewer and fewer, until at last there were hardly any at all.

"They go out under the curtain, and they don't come in again," said the girl called Sauna. Then she gave a whimper of horror, her eyes grew enormous and she cried, "Oh, I can see something *huge*—"

"Quiet, will you, for goodness' sake," said her aunt. "Thank heavens, there comes our blue case at last. You hold my handbag while I reach for it—"

But Sauna stood trembling uncontrollably for several minutes before she was able to obey her aunt's order.

People were so happy to find their luggage that they soon forgot about the big lumpy bags; nobody wasted any more time wondering who had sent them or who picked them up, or where they had gone to on that streaming wet Sunday in late September.

A couple of months went by before the first of the Cockatrices—for that was what they came to be called—made its appearance.

On a dark freezing December evening a truck driver called Sam Dwindle burst into his foreman's office looking very upset. He was white and sweating, and he shivered badly despite the thick jacket he wore.

"Yeah, yeah, I just know what you're going to say," he told the boss. "But listen to this: an hour ago when I was coming up the A3 from Portsmouth, on that new bit of bypass, I see this *Thing*, with big three-cornered flaps along its back and a tail the length of a tennis court and round ears that swivelled about like radar shields, and it was running along beside the motorway on its four fat legs. Running as fast as I was driving! And I was doing seventy—"

"Then you didn't ought to of been," said his boss, "not with a load of wineglasses. I suppose you'd put in a couple of hours at the George in Milford?"

"No, I hadn't, then," said the driver, injured. "I knew you wouldn't believe me. And if you don't, I'm sure I don't care. But I'm telling you, if that *Thing* had taken a fancy to cross the A3, instead of going off Dorking way, your truck would have been as flat as a Brillo pad and me with it.

"It had a tassel on its tail," he added. "And flaps there too."

"And a bow of pink ribbon on its head, I suppose," said his boss.

"OK, OK! You can give me my cards. If there's going to be things like that around, I'm going back to window-cleaning."

The next of the Cockatrices was sighted by a school botany class, who were out on the moor near the town of Appleby-under-Scar, two hundred miles to the north of the first occurrence. They were hunting for rabbit and deer tracks in the snow.

Two boys, Fred and Colin, had run on ahead of the rest, but they came racing back to the main group as fast as their legs would carry them.

"Miss! Come and see! There's a dinosaur in Hawes Dell."

"Now what moonshine have you got in your heads?" remarked the teacher, Miss Frobisher. But the whole class hurried up to the lip of the dell and looked down into it.

"Gracious me! Somebody must be making a film," said Miss Frobisher. "But that's not an *ordinary* dinosaur, Colin. It's a, it's, um, Tyrannosaurus Rex. You can tell that from its teeth and claws. The claws are at least eight inches long, and the teeth—"

"Will it bite us?" nervously asked a girl called Lily.

"No, dear. It's only a model, a very clever one indeed. I wonder where the cameramen are, and the film technicians. Dear me, what a lot it must have cost to make a model that size."

"It's coming this way," said Fred.

"Coo, it doesn't half stink," said Colin. "Like a whole truckload of rotting seaweed. Are you *sure* it's only a model, Miss?"

"Now, Colin! Use your intelligence! You know there

aren't dinosaurs about any more. They lived millions of years ago."

"Look at its tracks in the snow," said Lily. "Aren't they huge? Listen to it pant. Miss, I'm scared. I want to go home."

"Don't be a baby, Lily," said the teacher. "Just when you've got a chance to study this very clever model, which must be radio-controlled. Now you can see what it would have been like to live millions of years ago—"

Those were her last words.

The newspapers carried the story of the mysterious disappearance of Miss Frobisher and her class. "Their tracks were traced as far as the top of Hawes Dell," reported the *Appleby Herald*, "but heavy snow falling soon after prevented the police from discovering where they had gone after that. A local farmer, James Robson, claims to have seen what he described as a 'mammoth footprint' in the snow, but there has been no confirmation of his suggestion that some large beast was responsible for the strange fatality. Mr. Adrian Mardle, Chief Constable of West Humberland, is in charge of the case."

The next sighting was by an old lady, Mrs. Ada Backit, who lived in a high-rise apartment block in Glasgow, two hundred miles north-east of Appleby.

"Eh, Hannah," she said to her daughter, who had come in to cook her supper, "there's a face at the window looking in!"

"Och, come on, Ma, be your age," said Hannah, from the kitchenette where she was cooking fish fingers. "How can there be a face at the window when we're thirty floors up? Unless it's an angel wanting to watch *Neighbours?*"

"There's a face," repeated the old lady obstinately. "I can see its two big sad eyes the size o' porridge plates. I'm going to—"

Then there was silence. Hannah, walking in next minute with the dish of fish fingers, found nobody in the room.

"It was quite a shock to me," she reported that evening on local television, "because there is no other way out of the room. So where could Mum have gone? The window was shut and locked, and the flat is thirty storeys up."

QUEER DISAPPEARANCE OF GREAT-GRAND-MOTHER, the newspapers called it.

Then there was the business of the Christmas tree at Chiddinglea.

The residents had, as usual, erected a twenty-metre tree in the middle of the village green and decorated it with lights, tinsel, and coloured fruit. On Christmas Eve a party was always held on the green organized by the chairman of the Tree Committee, Colonel Clandon. Carols were sung, the lights were lit, and the whole village danced hand-in-hand round the tree.

"Hey!" called the boy named Michael, pausing to stare up at the star-filled sky. "Hey, look! There's something up there!"

Three or four people heard him and gazed up likewise. They saw that the stars were being blotted out by what seemed like a huge inky cloud. From this cloud something hung down which swept in circles with a faint whistling sound. And, from the very centre of the blackness, two great pale luminous eyes glared down at the revellers. Suddenly, with a loud sucking snap, the Christmas tree was uprooted from its fastenings; it flew upwards like a pin raised by a magnet.

Gasps and yells of indignation and fright rose among the dancers.

"Hey! What's going on?" "Put back our tree!" "What kind of joke is this?"

"If it's that aerial club from Wormfleet with their helicopter—" began Colonel Clandon, but he said no more.

The carol singers at Chiddinglea, like the schoolchildren of Appleby, vanished for ever, sucked upwards into the dark like spilt sugar into a vacuum cleaner.

Very soon the population of the British Isles had become noticeably smaller.

Cars stood around without drivers. Houses appeared to be empty. Bus queues were very much shorter. Babies' prams had no occupants. High streets of towns were empty and silent at midday.

In five years, half the country had become a desert. Buildings had fallen, or been knocked flat. The whole of London had gone underground. People didn't dare venture out in daylight any more. Shops were hidden in cellars. Parliament sat in a dungeon under the Tower of London. Schools were held in crypts. Even the Royal Family lived in the basement, which was all that remained of Buckingham Palace.

"Things can't go on like this much longer, Harold," said Lord Ealing, the Prime Minister, to General Grugg-Pennington, the Minister of Defence.

"No, they won't," agreed the defence minister. "Soon there won't be anybody left at all."

The two men were sitting on deckchairs on the Piccadilly Line, westbound, in Leicester Square tube station. Nobody else was there.

"I wonder where the monsters all come from in the first place?" mused Lord Ealing. "None of our scientists seem to agree about that. Do you suppose they can all have grown up from some nasty bacillus? Or mutated . . . ?"

"Oh, who cares where they came from? The point is that very soon they will have the whole country to themselves. The Snarks are the worst," said General Grugg-Pennington with a shiver.

"How can you tell? You've never seen a Snark."

"Of course I haven't! Everybody knows that if you see a Snark you vanish."

"I'd rather vanish than be munched up by a Flying Hammerhead."

"Remember that football match between Ipswich and Nottingham Forest?"

"Hammerhead got the goalie just as he was going to make a beautiful save," sighed the prime minister. "That was the last match played above ground."

The two men sat in silence for a while. Then Lord Ealing said, "Harold, I want you to set up a Cockatrice Corps."

People had fallen into the habit of calling *all* the creatures Cockatrices. There were too many kinds to remember their individual names: Kelpies, Telepods, Bycorns and Gorgons, Footmonsters, Brontotheres, Shovel-tuskers, Glyptodonts, Bonnacons, Cocodrills, Peridexions, Basilisks, Manticores, Hydras, Trolls, Sphynxes, and Chichivaches. And, worst of all, the deadly Mirkindole.

The country was completed infested with monsters. They had grown and multiplied, interbred and increased as fast as tadpoles in a pond.

So far as could be ascertained, the British Isles seemed to be the only territory at present affected by this disaster. Strict quarantine regulations, hastily put into effect, had up to now protected European, African, transatlantic countries, and the Antipodes.

Various attempts to end the siege of the infested islands by means of long-range missiles had proved wholly ineffective. The missiles simply melted before arriving at their targets.

The situation seemed hopeless.

"A Cockatrice Corps?" repeated the defence minister doubtfully. "But what about transport? How would they get about the country?"

"By rail."

"Underground? I do not think that would be feasible."

"No, we shall construct a special armour-plated train capable of running above ground."

"But what fuel will it use?"

Stocks of oil, coal, and gas had long ago been exhausted. People had to manage without.

"The train will run on wind power. Or maybe solar energy. Or stellar energy. There's plenty of that."

"Better than solar," said the general. "The monsters raise too much dust by day."

This was true. Monsters flying in swarms over the dry bare ground raised such thick clouds of dust that the sun was hardly ever seen and, even before fuel had run out, aircraft had to stop flying; the dust got into their compressor blades and the engines caught fire.

"And wind power," said Lord Ealing. "There's plenty of that. Or diesel bricks."

"Hmn, a wind-powered, armour-plated train. That *might* be a possibility . . ."

"All the old tracks are still there, so far as we know," pointed out Lord Ealing.

"Gregory Clipspeak would be a good man to put in charge of the corps. But it would be a most dangerous mission. We'd have to call for volunteers."

"You'd get plenty. People are fed up with living underground."

"Very well," said the defence minister. "I'll set up an operations room at once."

And that was how the Cockatrice Corps came into being.

While the engine of the *Cockatrice Belle* was being lovingly assembled by skilled volunteers in London, the food shortage in some northern towns was becoming more and more severe.

"It's not a case of tightening belts," said the Provost of Manchester. "It's got down to eating them."

One November day the Hempfields District Emergency Warden took a look at his afternoon's agenda, and saw that he was due to pay a call on a Mrs. Florence Monsoon at number fifteen, Brylcreme Court. This was a melancholy, run-down council block, and number fifteen was on the fifth floor, up five flights of battered concrete stairs. Dashed over the staircase walls were various dramatic portrayals of monsters executed in spray paint, but these had been done several years before, when the monsters were still a novelty; now the pictures had faded, as had the enthusiasm for doing them, and the supply of spray paint had long since run out, and the artists had, many of them, been swallowed by the monsters so the walls beyond the third and fourth storeys were mostly undecorated. And there were no pictures at all on the corridor walls leading to Mrs. Monsoon's front door. But an inscription very low down (as if it had been done by a dwarf or a four-year-old child) read: "Mrs. F——Monsoon is an old witch."

The warden, whose name was Mr. Mossready, shook his head at this as he lifted the metal knocker on the door and gave it a couple of sharp raps. (Electric bells in Manchester had long since ceased to function.)

After his knock there followed a long suspicious silence inside the flat, though Mr. Mossready felt fairly certain that he could hear someone moving around inside, and a woman talking in a low voice.

He rapped again.

By and by, he became aware that he was being observed through the tiny glass spy-hole by a hostile pale-grey eye.

" 'Oo's that?" snapped a voice.

"The warden."

"How do I know you're what you say? There's all sorts about these days."

For answer he held his warden's badge up to the spy-hole and, after another extended unfriendly pause, the door was very slowly drawn open. Inside stood a thin scraggy woman with a long pale face, grey hair done in a bun on top, and a grey apron, which had once been white, tied over a lot of cardigans worn in layers, like onion skins.

"Mrs. Florence Monsoon?"

" 'Oo else'd be living here?" she demanded.

"Who else *is* living here? That's what I want to know. You applied for an extra ration of carrots for your niece Sauna Blow. Where did she come from? There was no niece mentioned before, when the ration cards for meat and bread were issued."

"She don't eat no meat nor bread. Only carrots."

"Why?"

"That's her business, ain't it? Oh well, s'pose you best come in, don't need to have the whole building sticking their noses into my affairs," grumbled the woman, giving a sharp glance up and down the empty corridor, as if elephants' ears extended, quivering, from every closed door.

The warden followed her through a lobby about the size of a chair seat into a very small living room. In the middle of the room was a card-table covered with a hairy brown cloth, and on top of that one of yellowed lace; round the table were crammed four chairs with red velour seats; the walls were covered by display shelves, and in each corner but one there were triangular chiffonieres; the fourth corner held a dead television set, and the rest of the space was taken up by small coffee-tables with spindly legs. On all of these stood a multitude of tiny china mugs and jugs, each with an inscription from some seaside resort: "A Present from Margate," "A Present from Blackpool," "A Present from Ryde." There must have been thousands of them. It seemed that Mrs. Monsoon had been busy dusting them, for she held a piece of rag, which she now tucked into her waistband in a martyred manner. A brown-tile fireplace held a paper fan in a jam jar, and a small potted palm stood on the window-sill, blocking off any light.

Dusting all those little things must take a tremendously long time, thought Mr. Mossready, tired at the very thought. All day, most likely every day.

"Well?" snapped Mrs. Monsoon. "What nosy-parkering set of Paul Prys sent *you* along here?"

"Food Rationing and Public Security."

"Public Security, huh! Not much of that these days."

Mr. Mossready displayed his badge again, and drew out a long form like a scroll, which he had wrapped round a dead ballpoint pen.

But while he did so his eyes were fixed in fascinated disapproval on the girl who sat motionless at the opposite side of the card-table, with her back to the window.

The reason she couldn't move was that her hands were tied tightly with strips of rag to the back of her chair, one on each side.

Her cheeks were extremely pale. Her red hair was done neatly in two plaits. She gave Mr. Mossready a weary glance, but said nothing. She did sniff a little, though, as if she would have liked to blow her nose. The warden wondered if she had been crying, or if she had a cold.

"Are you Sauna Aslauga Blow?" he asked, consulting his form. "Daughter of Ted and Emily Blow of Newcastle-upon-Tyne?"

"Yes, sir."

"Your parents are dead, and Mrs. Florence Monsoon is your guardian?"

"Yes, sir," she said again sadly. "That's right."

"What relation is she to you?"

"Father's cousin," put in Mrs. Monsoon.

"Why, might I ask, do you keep the child tied up?"

At this the girl's eyes flew nervously to the woman.

"Well! What a question!" said Mrs. Monsoon acidly. "I should have thought *any* fool could see the reason for *that*. The child's so active and restless, the very first day she was here she smashed eleven of my precious souvenirs. Naturally I wasn't having any more of that; so, since then, except at mealtimes—which she takes in the kitchen—she has to have her hands tied."

Mr. Mossready glanced at the kitchen, which he could see from where he stood. (He had not been invited to sit down. In fact there would scarcely have been room.) The kitchen was the same size as the front hall, with sink, stove, and cupboard arranged round the sides of a standing space.

"Mrs. Monsoon, how long has the child been living with you?"

"Five years. Ever since her mum and dad was killed in an air crash in Spain. Just before the Troubles, that was."

Sauna was heard to sniff again.

"*Why* does she not eat meat and bread? (If available.) Is she on a special diet? A vegetarian?"

"Meat an' bread'd make her too active, wouldn't they?" demanded Mrs. Monsoon. "There'd be no holding her, once she'd gobbled a lot of stuff like that. So that's why I put in for extra carrots."

"Do you like carrots?" the warden asked Sauna. She nodded, resignedly.

"Oh, very well. In the circumstances I am prepared to allow the application." He made a tick on his form. "Does the child ever get out?"

"I don't see as that's any of your business," said Mrs. Monsoon coldly. "But, yes, she does, when there ain't too many Snarks about."

"And how long do you expect to have her residing with you? Does she have any other friends . . . relatives . . . people to care for her? If something should happen to you?" the warden said delicately.

Mr. Mossready was not one for rushing in where angels fear to tread. But he did feel this arrangement was highly unsatisfactory.

The child looked so very pale and glum.

When he said "other friends" something slightly odd appeared to happen to Mrs. Florence Monsoon.

The pupils of her pale-grey eyes dilated and began to shine, as if they were made from small blobs of mercury.

She stared at the warden for a few minutes, without answering.

He looked into her eyes, lulled into a kind of waking trance by the bright points of light in their pupils. It seemed to him that he could hear a shrill, tiny voice, like that of a gnat or mosquito, which whined plaintively somewhere up above him near the curtain rail:

"I don't like it here! How much longer do I have to stay in this airless ugliness? When can I rejoin my friends? Abiron, Asmodeus, Belial, Chamoth—when can we play together again? In air? In air and darkness? I was not told that I would have to hover here in a trap—in a trap, in a trap, in a horrible trap—"

The voice ended in a batlike squeak.

"I beg your pardon? What did you say?"

Mr. Mossready was exceedingly startled, and more than a little scared. The child had not spoken, he'd be prepared to swear; her lips were pressed tightly together, and she had been looking down at the yellow lace cover on the brown hairy tablecloth.

But the voice had not seemed to come from the woman either; could he possibly have imagined it? A voice up there above his head? Near the dead electric light bulb in its fringed lampshade?

Mrs. Monsoon was still gazing at the warden in a strange sightless manner, her eyes like two silver nail-heads fastening something down in her blank face.

Now the girl spoke.

"It's just Aunt Floss's hearing-aid, sir; it does go like that sometimes. So does the kettle. It's—it's just the airwaves round here. Aunt doesn't hear ordinary sounds so well when it's like that. But—but, I don't mind it *so* much here, you see, I'm waiting—I'm hoping—"

"Hoping for what, child?"

"Hoping for my cousin Dakin to come along," explained the girl. "He's way off still, but I'm pretty sure he *will* come, by and by—" She was talking very fast and softly, with a wary eye on her aunt.

Mrs. Monsoon suddenly gave her head a quick, angry shake.

"Cousin? Whatever are you talking about, you silly girl?" she snapped. "Hoping for your cousin Dakin, indeed! I'd like to know what use he'd be! He's only a bit of a lad, somewhere down there in London, probably et up long ago by a Terrapod. Don't take notice of the child, Mr. Mossy, she talks a right lot of nonsense at times. Gets silly notions in her head. It's all I can do to keep my patience with her."

The woman's eyes were normal again now, her pupils dark, the same as anybody else's might be. And the bat-like squeaking voice—from a radio speaker, could it have been, except who had a radio these days?—was silent.

Quickly, uneasily, Mr. Mossready rolled up the public health form again, nodded at the two inmates of the flat and stepped back towards the entrance door.

". . . *When can my friends come and play?*" whined the tiny voice.

Hurriedly—not far from panic—Mr. Mossready stepped out of the front door and slammed it behind him. Standing in the passage, he thought he heard Mrs. Monsoon's angry exclamation, "*Hush!* Not yet! I've told you over and over!"

There's something downright peculiar, not at all what it should be, about the set-up in that place, ruminated Mr. Mossready, making for the staircase. But what can *I* do? *Nothing's* as it should be, these days. I'm sorry for that poor child, though.

As he reached the stairhead, a fat woman was struggling slowly up. He could hear her puffing and wheezing while she climbed the last flight, so he waited politely on the top step.

"You just been visiting Mrs. Monsoon?" asked the woman as she came level with the warden and paused to get her breath. "She's at home then, is she?"

"Yes, she is," said the warden, hoping to get a little more information about that forlorn child. "Er—are you a friend of Mrs. Monsoon?"

"Ow, no, no, Mister—not to say a *friend*," declared the fat woman hastily. "More of an acquaintance, like. A neighbour. She gives readings, you know, Mrs. M does—cards, dreams, tea-leaves. She's from up north, in Scotland, see, where the nights are so long they can all see in the dark. Clear-seeing, they calls it. Mrs. Monsoon can scry, like." Then growing nervous, wondering if she had been indiscreet, she added, "Not in a crystal ball, don't get me wrong, Mister, nothink of that gipsyish sort, no funny business, and *never* for money—she reads hands, see, gives advice. It's all *ever* so ladylike and refined. Nothink nasty, nothink nasty at all, money never changes hands—"

Wouldn't be much good if it did, reflected the Warden. Money had long since ceased to be of any importance or use.

The woman pushed hurriedly past him, leaving a strong aroma of garlic behind her.

"Does the child help her?" asked Mr. Mossready.

The disapproval in his voice made the fat woman even more nervous.

"No, not to say *help*, Mister—not to say help. Oh dear me, no, that wouldn't be legal, would it? But, of course, she's *there*, in the room; can't help that, can she, if she sometimes lets fall a word or two. She gotta speak sometimes, don't she? Truth to tell, she can see through walls, at times, that kid can. Useful gift, ain't it? Wouldn't mind having the knack myself, right handy it'd be when the rent collector comes a-calling for his ten pairs of hand-knitted socks!" She laughed wheezily, then gave Mr. Mossready a cautious glance, trying to guess his reason for being there. "Well, we all got to do the best we can for each other, these awful times, don't we?" she added vaguely.

She waddled off along the passage towards Mrs. Monsoon's door. Staring after her uneasily, Mr. Mossready noticed for the first time that she had a dog with her. Or had it been there, lurking outside in the passage, all the time? Or—*was* it a dog? Something smallish, about the size of an Aberdeen terrier, scuttled along the corridor, keeping close to the angle of the wall.

Maybe I'm coming down with the flu, thought Mr. Mossready, rubbing his brow; they say there's a real nasty virus going about, affects your hearing, makes you think you hear bird calls and cats mewling, makes you think you see peculiar things that aren't properly there. For I could have sworn that what I saw scurrying along the passage was not a dog but a *face*, running on six legs and looking up at me with a nasty grin as it went.

What I need's a nice cup of hot turnip tea to go with my mint and parsley sandwich.

Reassuring himself Mr. Mossready patted his jacket pocket, and for a second time wiped his brow, which was covered with a shimmer of sweat. I'll be right glad to get out of Brylcreme Court. The ventilation in this building is very poor, and that's a fact. Nasty odours about, something like rotten eggs with a dash of hot melted metal in there as well.

So Mr. Mossready was decidedly put out at being waylaid again, down in the lobby, by yet another stranger. You'd think, from its look, that this building was mostly deserted, he thought, rubbish scattered all over the floor, no proper maintenance, peeling paint everywhere, so quiet you could hear an ant hiccup, yet there seem to be a lot of odd bods about.

The man who now intercepted the warden at the foot of the stairs could certainly be described as an odd bod. He was extremely thin and pale, so thin that his face looked like a skull. A cowlick of lank hair hung down over his white bony brow, and two doleful mud-coloured eyes peered about as if they had never seen anything to interest or please them, and never expected to.

The man wore a kind of grey canvas uniform and carried a nasty-looking tool, part spade, part bill-hook, part cleaver.

"Afternoon, sir," he addressed Mr. Mossready politely enough. "I reckon it's just about afternoon, n'now, eh? Sun's climbed as high as it's going to, would you say?" He gave a sniff at his own flight of fancy.

"Noon to ye," mumbled Mr. Mossready, wishing the man would step out of the way and let him go by, into the fresh air.

"Now I wonder, sir," said the man without budging. "I see you are an emergency warden, sir, I see it by your badge— I wonder if by any chance you would have been calling on Mrs. Florence Monsoon?"

"Now why should you think that?" snapped Mr. Mossready, not at all pleased at being interrogated about his professional pursuits by this scruffy stranger.

"It's just, sir, that, to the best of my knowledge, Mrs. Monsoon is the only resident of this building, these days. Unless, of course, you were inspecting the block so as to condemn it as unfit for human habitation?"

The mud-coloured eyes were fixed searchingly on Mr. Mossready's face.

"No; that is not my function," said the warden. "Anyhow, compared with some, this building's not too bad. Who are *you*, may I ask?" he added, still wishing the man would move out of his way.

"Tom Flint, sir, dog operative. Under the latest regula-

tions, section Twenty-two-B of clause seventy-nine, Func-
tions of local government officials, fifteen August last year, I
am empowered to search out and destroy any unclaimed do-
mestic canines—"

"Oh, is that so, yes, yes, I see—" interrupted Mr. Mossready, still trying to get past. "Excellent, very proper, can't
have unclaimed mongrels roaming all over the city—"

"And you tell me that you have recently made a professional call on Mrs. Florence Monsoon, sir, and that you
would say she had no resident canine pet in her apartment?"

"I *didn't* say that I had called on Mrs. Monsoon," con-
tended Mr. Mossready peevishly. "But, as it happens, I was
in her place—and not greatly impressed by the state of affairs
there. I may say—" he went on, more to himself than to the
other man, "the child seemed very much in the dumps; don't
care to see a young 'un kept under restraint like that."

"A child? The occupant of number fifteen has a child residing with her?" inquired Tom Flint. His tone, which had
been rather vague, now turned quite sharp.

"What concern is that of yours, pray?" snapped Mr. Mossready, still trying to edge past the dog operative, who had a
dank, musty, sweaty odour about him, which combined most
unpleasantly with the stuffy atmosphere of Brylcreme Court.

"Why—kiddies and dogs go together—don't they? You
get a kiddy in a flat, nine times out o' ten you get a puppy
too—or a kitten, or a hamster, or one o' they canary birds.
And pets *breed*, you know, one thing leads to another, before
you know where you are, there's a whole drawerful of white
mice, a kennel full of tykes, or half a dozen moggies; something that's clean against present-day regulations. Now—to
save me trouble, sir—would you declare as you had seen
nothing of that nature in Mrs. Monsoon's place?"

"No . . . oo . . . ." said Mr. Mossready, a little uncertainly.

Tom Flint pounced.

"Ah hah! There *was* summat dicey? Not quite as it should be? You smelt cats, maybe—or heard birds a-tweeting?"

"No, I didn't. No, I did not. Nothing like that. But there was a queer voice . . ."

Mr. Mossready wished more and more that he could get away from this annoying interruption and find a quiet place to eat his parsley sandwich and get a cup of something hot.

"A parrot, maybe?" suggested Tom Flint. "Parrots can do funny tricks with their voices?"

"No. No. Nothing like that," Mr. Mossready repeated. "Just a voice. The radio, perhaps."

He scowled at the other man, waiting for him to say that since there was no mains electricity in Manchester, and batteries were not to be had, he could have heard no radio.

"I tell you what I did see," he suddenly—to his own amazement—found himself volunteering. "I saw a face, running along on legs. Right nasty, it looked."

"Ah. A face on legs." Tom Flint greeted this statement without the slightest surprise. "So. Where was that, then?"

"Up yonder." Mr. Mossready waved to the staircase. "Outside Mrs. Monsoon's place. Maybe it came with the woman who was calling on her."

"A face on legs . . . Did it have a collar?" Flint asked.

"I saw none. Right nasty it was," Mr. Mossready repeated. "Had a spiteful grin. Made me feel queer."

Tom Flint surveyed him.

"What you need," he said in an unexpected tone of friendly sympathy, "is a herbal doughnut and a mug of hot rhubarb wine. And I know just the place to go for that."

This seemed such an attractive programme that Mr. Mossready felt inclined to ignore his first mistrust of the man who suggested it.

"That does sound champion," he said. "Would it be far from here, though? I've another three calls to make in this area."

"Nay, not a step. Just round the corner. A gaffer I know has his own stall down by the Ship Canal. I'll show you, just you come with me. He brews his own rhubarb wine—fresh-picked rhubarb that grows in the ruins of the town hall—I've had it many a time, and I can tell you, it's better than *tea!*"

"Tea!" sighed Mr. Mossready, following with docility as his companion led the way round the street corner and along a narrow alleyway between piles of rubble, and so down to the towpath where the canal ran greasily between huge ruined buildings.

"There—d'ye see—along there?"

Sure enough, Mr. Mossready did think he saw a makeshift stall, built from old bits of lath and galvanized iron. And behind its ramshackle counter a man was boiling a kettle over what looked like a Bunsen burner. The flame of the burner flickered between the stallholder and his customers; Mr. Mossready could see nothing of him but a vague misty shape.

"Tansy tea or hot rhubarb punch?" he asked in a low creaking voice as they came alongside the counter.

"Tea for me, punch for my mate," Flint told him.

Two thick china mugs were filled with steaming fluid.

Mossready was preparing to take a sip when Flint stopped him.

"Nay, man, that's not the way. Inhale a grand sniff of the steam first. That will relax the coats of the stomach. Hold your nozzle right over—that's the way—and breathe in, hard. Once, twice—three times . . ."

Tom Flint and the shadowy figure behind the counter watched with calm interest as Mr. Mossready inhaled his third breath and began to stagger uncertainly across the towpath.

"Feels like you can hear the music of the spheres a-whirling round your head, don't it?" said Tom Flint in a quiet, solicitous tone, and he gave Mr. Mossready a sharp push between the shoulderblades which sent him plunging into the canal.

Just before the waters closed over his head for ever, Mr. Mossready heard Tom Flint ask, in a pleading tone, "Did I do well, Master?"

But what the answer was, if, indeed, one came, the warden did not hear.

Chapter two

The last recruit to the Cockatrice Corps was a drummer boy, Dakin Prestwich. When he told his mother that he had been accepted for the anti-monster corps she burst into floods of tears.

"Oh, Dakin, you never! What d'you want to go and do *that* for? You must be out of your finitical mind!"

"I'm sick of living in the strong room of Barclays Bank, Shepherd's Bush," said Dakin. "I want to see some daylight."

"You'll be killed for sure! You'll be crunched up by a Flying Hammerhead. Or stamped on by a Footmonster. Or the deadly Mirkindole will get you. And I shall be left all alone," wept Mrs. Prestwich.

"Except for Mrs. Monk, Mrs. Prateman, Miss Jeppardy, Frau Fischer, Fräulein Gross, Mr. Teal, and Mrs. Widsey," pointed out Dakin. These were the other people with whom Dakin and his mother shared the strong room of the bank.

Several of them had been very kind to him, lent him books to read and taught him German, but now he wanted a change.

"You just don't care about your poor old mother."

"Yes, I do, Ma. And I'll be all right. They're going to give us Snark glasses, and there'll be radio advance warning on the train, and a ballista for firing red-hot missiles at the Mirkindole. I'll come back safe and sound—you'll see—and maybe I'll be able to bring you a few dandelion leaves or a bit of wild spinach."

People were absolutely starved for greenery because they never dared to go into the open country. All the food came from tins.

"Those Snark glasses are no use," wailed Mrs. Prestwich. "They say you can only use them six times. After that you see the Snark through them and vanish away."

"I'll be all right," repeated Dakin. Then he hugged his mother and left, because he could see that no amount of argument would ever convince her.

The troop train was waiting for its crew in a huge pillared hall underneath King's Cross Station.

The *Cockatrice Belle*, as it came to be called, had been constructed with tremendous care and enthusiasm. People were so happy to do anything that might rid the land of monsters that they had been prepared to work all hours of the day and night. Hundreds of willing helpers had toiled for weeks in relays; the train had been built from all the bits and pieces left over from buildings that had been smashed by the devouring invaders: mahogany from grand restaurants, brass from pubs, velvet from theatres. Everybody brought something. Fishermen brought hooks, old ladies brought scissors and needles, children brought paint boxes and marbles.

The train was armour-plated in bronze, inlaid with gold stripes, and the windows were triple bullet-proof glass with

Snark-proof shades that could be automatically lowered at the touch of a button in the operations coach. On the roof were the wind-vanes and a row of solar-energy panels, in case the sun ever shone, to supplement the stellar power. The wheels were steel with rubber suction tyres. Tanks of concentrated diesel bricks hung suspended beneath the train.

Dakin Prestwich ran up to the uniformed sergeant who kept guard at the ticket gate. He saluted smartly.

"Drummer-boy Prestwich reporting for duty, sir," he said.

"Ho!" snorted the sergeant, who was tall and stringy and red-faced. "I wonder why Colonel Clipspeak saw fit to recruit a little chitty-faced object like *you*, when there was plenty others to choose from?"

"It's because I play the drum real psychedelic," said Dakin.

"Speak when you're spoke to! And you address me as Sergeant. Sergeant Bellswinger I am, but Sergeant's enough for you."

"Yes, Sergeant."

"You get along to the boot-car, that's your station. Corporal Dwindle will issue you with uniform and tell you your duties. And don't let me hear that drum," added the Sergeant, scowling with great disfavour at Dakin's enormous instrument. "Don't let me hear that drum *ever*, unless orders comes as it's to be sounded, or the Colonel will do his nut."

"How can I practise, then?" said Dakin, dismayed.

"None of your lip. Double along to the boot-car."

Sergeant Bellswinger turned to bark at a new group of recruits, or rookies, and Dakin went along to the far end of the train.

Corporal Dwindle, a sad, scoop-faced man, issued Dakin with his uniform, which was dark brown, the colour of plain chocolate, with gold buttons.

"And here's a pair of Snark glasses, which have to be greased every day with Vaseline, and a compass, a walkie-talkie, and a liquid-air pistol," said the corporal, handing Dakin these items. "Write your name on the receipt form here, please. I'll be giving you instructions how to use the pistol; meantime, don't go fooling about with it. You can stack your drum up there in the rack. Your duties are as follows: at seven ack emma every morning you take the colonel his early-morning tea from the galley—"

"Where do I find the colonel?"

"In his private coach, that's past the table tennis car and before you get to the video van. After the colonel's had his tea, you polish the boots of all officers and NCOs. Then you cleans the windows," said the corporal, his eyes lighting with enthusiasm because he had once been a window-cleaner himself.

"What? *All* of them?"

"Every one. And I want to see them glitter."

"Every day I have to do that?"

"Every blessed day. Visibility has to be kept at a maximum. When that's done you takes the colonel and officers their mid-morning coffee."

"I reckon they won't get their coffee till tea-time," said Dakin, looking along the length of the train at the rows of glass panes.

There were twenty-two coaches and an observation platform on the *Cockatrice Belle*. During the two weeks' training period that followed, before the Monster Brigade were allowed out on active service, Dakin learned the order of the cars by heart, backwards and forwards; every morning while he cleaned the windows he had to recite them to Corporal Dwindle.

"Engine cab—arsenal—broom cupboard—ops room—men's mess—galley—officers' mess—officers' quarters—video room—Colonel's cabin—table tennis car—ten privates' barracks—boot-car and the observation platform."

To help himself remember the order, Dakin took the initial letters E A B O M G O O V C T P P P P P P P P P P B and made a sentence from them: "Every agile boy outwits monsters. Grapple off, on very cold Tuesdays, Pythons, Peridexions, Pookas, seven Porcupines, and Basilisks."

The colonel's car and officers' rooms were handsomely furnished with Turkish carpets, mahogany couches, brass fittings, and potted palms. The men's carriages were much plainer, with slatted bunks that had to be folded back in the daytime, and the men were crowded ten to a compartment, whereas the colonel had a whole bedsitter coach to himself with armchairs, bookshelves, and a grand piano. The officers slept on folding beds in their spacious parlour, but there were only five of them—a major, two captains, two lieutenants—so at least they were better off than the privates.

"It doesn't seem fair," said Dakin to Corporal Dwindle, as he polished windows.

"Nobody asked your opinion," said Corporal Dwindle. But then he added, "Life ain't fair, take it or leave it. Why should my missus have got swallowed by a Hammerhead? She never did nothing wrong her whole life—only watched telly and knitted four hundred and seventy-two pairs of socks. Life ain't fair. You might as well get used to that."

Dakin went on polishing windows.

Meanwhile, up in Manchester, his cousin Sauna was leading a sad and suppressed existence. Polishing three hundred and twenty windows every day would have seemed a treat to her.

* * *

On the first morning of action, as soon as Ensign-Driver Catchpole blew the reveille on his engine whistle, Dakin shot out of his bunk in the boot-car, flung on his uniform, and dashed along the corridor to the galley, where he boiled a kettle on the brass hotplate and made a pot of tea for the colonel. He knew how, since he had often made tea for his mother, Mrs. Prateman, Miss Jeppardy, and the other people who lived in the Barclays Bank strong-room. Then he carried the tea on a tray to the colonel's cabin, tapped on the door, opened it, and went smartly in.

A brown face glared at him from under the royal-blue velvet counterpane—a face with glittering grey eyes, bristly white eyebrows, and long sweeping white moustaches.

"And what in the name of the Pink Panjandrum brought *you* in?" snarled the colonel, putting in a single eyeglass.

"Morning, sir. Drummer Dakin, sir, brought your tea, sir," said Dakin, and set the cup on the mahogany bed-pedestal.

After one sip, the colonel's eyebrows almost glided over the top of his bald head.

"You call this gnats' bathwater *tea?* What did you make it with?"

"Stewed dried grass, sir, like always."

Real tea had long since vanished from the British Isles.

"Well, you can take it and tell the mess orderly to wash dishes in it. Or his feet. From now on I'll make my own tea."

And the colonel pointed to an automatic tea-maker at the other side of his bed. It had a radio-controlled kettle which, just at this moment, blew out a puff of steam and then shot a neat jet of water into a small pot, while a bugle recording

played "It's great to get up in the morning." From the pot
floated a scent of brandy.

"Blow me!" said Dakin, greatly impressed.

"Neat, eh? Runs on batteries from the engine." The
colonel poured himself a cup of tar-coloured liquid. "Ahhhh!
That's better. Now run along, boy, and take my boots and
polish them till you can see your teeth in them. And don't
bring me any more of that hogwash tea."

"No, sir, thank you, sir."

At this time in Manchester Mrs. Florence Monsoon and her
niece Sauna were, like the other inhabitants of the city, living on thistledown tea and (when they could get it) dandelion root porridge. And they were burning up Sauna's old
schoolbooks for fuel.

"And it'll be those next," said Aunt Floss, casting a cov-
etous look at Sauna's twin teddybears.

"Oh, no! Please!"

"Well? What else have we got? You don't have any
dolls—do you?"

"N-no," said Sauna, trembling. "They got left behind in
Newcastle—"

Aunt Floss compressed her lips and continued to eye the
bears.

After two weeks of training it was announced to the Cockatrice Corps that the train would go out on a trial run the next
day.

"Where are we going?" Dakin asked Corporal Dwindle,
who was giving him instructions in how to clean his liquid-
air pistol.

"Manchester."

"Fancy!" said Dakin. "My Auntie Floss lives there. Or she did, before the Troubles began. O' course, I dunno if she's still alive now; she might have been et by a Hammerhead. After Dad died we stopped hearing from her. I went to Manchester once when I was a kid. It's a big place, ennit? I remember tall buildings and lots of buses."

"No buses there now, I don't suppose. And the people are all starving. That's why we're going—to take them supplies. There's a big colony of Snarks all around Manchester—got the town surrounded. The people built a town wall and dug a moat, but they're trapped inside. Been radioing for help. When they could raise a signal, that is."

"What provisions are we taking them?"

"Tinned carrots."

"I think I'd just as soon starve," said Dakin.

"I'd as soon starve as eat the muck they serve us in the mess," muttered Private Quillroy, stropping away at his Kelpie knife.

Everybody was grumbling about the food served in the mess.

"How are we supposed to fight Hammerheads and Shovel-tuskers on watery mash and goat soup?"

"The bangers taste of minced mud."

"The tapioca's nobbut ground up fibreglass."

"The wads are made of plasterboard."

"And lined with dental floss."

Still, despite complaints about the food, the whole troop were in high spirits when, for the first time, on the first of December, the *Cockatrice Belle* huffed and chuffed slowly backwards up the long ramp that led from the pillared chamber under King's Cross. A military band on the platform played Tosti's *Goodbye*. The Prime Minister, the Minister of

Defence, the Royal Family, and a large tearful crowd were left behind, waving flags made of old tea-cloths. Ensign-Driver Catchpole joyously tooted his whistle and the great glittering train crept gingerly into real daylight at last. It was all garlanded in tinsel and hung with small red and green glass bells, because Christmas was only a few weeks away.

"Coo!" breathed Dakin, blinking against the dazzle as he gazed out, but Sergeant Bellswinger roared over the inter-com: "Snark glasses—at the double—in *position!*" and they all clapped their protective spectacles on their noses. Behind the train the defensive gate clanged down over the mouth of the tunnel; the engine unhitched and rolled up a side track to the front of the train. Then it rehitched itself, and the *Cockatrice Belle* was on her way.

At first the landscape north of King's Cross was a bit of a disappointment to Dakin. For sixty miles nothing could be seen but pink and yellow rubble, great dusty piles of smashed houses. Gradually these were replaced by snow-scattered country—very *wild* country, with clumps of scrubby trees and bramble thickets, and tangly three-metre hedges, and huge ragged weeds on the railway embankments. It was all quite silent, except for the mild regular noise of the train, chunketa-chunketa-chunk, chunk, manunka-chunk, as it am-bled its way along the rusty rails.

Occasionally the shriek of a monster could be heard. And among the bushes monsters of every kind could be seen, lurking, prowling, flapping, fighting each other, or just star-ing at the train with huge glassy eyes as it slipped by.

"What about *bridges?*" General Grugg-Pennington had said to Lord Ealing, who replied peevishly, "How can we tell? Who knows what condition the bridges may be in? The men will have to survey and repair bridges when they come to them, if necessary under covering fire from the train."

Luckily the bridges during the first part of the journey, as far as Oxford, were found to be in a fair condition; the *Cockatrice Belle* passed over them safely, gliding at a cautious twenty miles per hour.

Meanwhile the men of the troop had their hands full. Many monsters attacked the train. Flying Hammerheads swooped down from above, their ugly jaws snapping and scooping, and were fought off with flame-throwers and cross-bows; great herds of Griffins, Footmonsters, Cocodrills, and Shovel-tuskers roamed beside the permanent way, often crossing the rails, snapping and slashing and clawing at the men as they battled to clear the track. Progress was often exasperatingly slow.

"Still," as Corporal Dwindle said to Sergeant Bellswinger towards the evening of the first day, "every little helps, and we must have done in quite a few of the brutes. The men are getting used to 'em."

"Pity Private Quillroy had to go and get swallowed by that Shovel-tusker. If only he'd studied his drill and remembered to hold his crossbow sideways on—"

"Ah well," said Corporal Dwindle, "at least it's a lesson to the others. Now do you see," he told Dakin, "why you got to keep those windows crystal clear? We need all the view we can get."

"Beg parding, Sergeant!" exclaimed Private Bundly, coming into the men's mess, where Dakin was cleaning the windows and the two NCOs were taking a cup of tea. "Beg parding, but we've found a stowaway in the arsenal. Hid away at the back behind a stack of December guns, she was."

"*She?*" demanded Bellswinger wrathfully. "And who the blazes may *she* be?"

"Here she be, Ser'nt," said Private Bundly, and he pushed into the mess cabin a rather strange figure, at first hardly recognizable as a person, for it was all tied up in sacks. However when these were removed, they saw a lanky, melancholy-looking, grey-haired woman wearing a homespun skirt, leather kneeboots, and a man's forage jacket.

"Why the pize was she wearing all those sacks?"

"To make herself look like a bundle of hammunition, I reckon."

"The colonel will have to see her. Come along, you!" Bellswinger roared at the woman, who seemed too alarmed to speak; and he led her to the cabin of the colonel, who was playing waltzes on his grand piano.

Dakin followed inquisitively. Dusk had fallen by now, and he didn't see the point of cleaning windows if you couldn't see out anyway. He stood in the cabin doorway looking in.

"A *stowaway*? A *female* stowaway? On my train?" The colonel was scandalized. "What's your name, woman? What d'you mean by it? Why in the name of blue ruin did you *do* it?"

The stowaway seemed to pick up a bit of courage in the colonel's presence. She looked at the grand piano and drew a disapproving finger over the dust on its lid.

"Oh, if you please, sir, my name's Mrs. Churt and I hid under all those pepper-grinders, or whatever they are, because I *did* so long to get a glimpse of anything green. I used to have a little garden, sir, before all these horrible Griffins and Footmonsters and Bonnacons come along. We lived out past Blackheath way, and I grew lettuce and Canterbury bells and radishes, and I can't *abide* living all my life in the dark like a blessed earwig, sir! That was why I done it!"

"Well, but, my good woman, other people have to put up with living underground; and so must you. There's no *room* for you on this train. We'll be obliged to stop, you know, and put you off."

"Beg pardon, sir," muttered Lieutenant Upfold in an undertone from the doorway. "Know it ain't my place to speak, but the old lady wouldn't last ten minutes if you put her out here. There's a deuce of a lot of Basilisks about. You can *smell* 'em—like wet washing, don't you know?"

"I don't need *you* to teach me my business, thank you, Upfold," snapped the colonel, but Mrs. Churt fell on her knees and clasped her hands and cried, "Oh, please, please, sir, don't put me off! I can cook—my old Churt, what was took by a Telepod, he used to say I was a real grade-one cook, the best in Kent—and I have useful Dreams, sir, often—and I can make drinks for the lads, and cakes and that, and give 'em little treats, like those Vivandeers used to in the Foreign Legiron. And I could make you a cross-stitch cover for your piano sir, to keep the dust off it."

"Humph! What kind of Dreams?" demanded the Colonel, who had been attracted, though he would not admit it, by the offer of the cross-stitch cover.

"Dreams, like, that show which way to go, if there's a question about it."

"Well, that's as may be. I'll think about it. Overnight. In the meantime," Colonel Clipspeak told the sergeant, "you had best lock the woman in the broom cupboard. Is it true, Sergeant, that the men have been grumbling about the catering?"

"Can't say as to that, sir," said the sergeant stiffly.

"That in the officers' mess leaves everything to be desired," murmured Lieutenant Upfold.

Sergeant Bellswinger hustled Mrs. Churt away, but Dakin, lingering, whispered urgently, "Sir! The food's horrible! Soup made of melted boot polish. And the spuds are like summat that's been dug up."

"Potatoes *are* dug up, you idiotic boy."

"No, sir. I knows better than that. They comes out of tins."

In two days Mrs. Churt was cooking for the entire troop, both officers and men. Her vegetable stews were mouthwatering, so were her steamed puddings, rich, crumbly, and wreathed in strawberry jam. Her doughnuts were light as thistledown, her raisin cake was satisfyingly stodgy.

Mess Orderly Widgery, who had been doing the cooking, was sent back to grease December guns in the arsenal, and Mrs. Churt presided over the galley. She had green fingers too: she started to grow little slips of parsley and chives in jam jars, she polished the colonel's potted palm with salad oil, and she rescued the drooping geraniums in the officers' parlour from an early death.

And her cross-stitch cover for the colonel's piano was immediately put in hand and grew inch by inch.

Dakin soon became very fond of Mrs. Churt. He would sit in the galley, sometimes of an evening, practising his drum-taps on a tea-cloth stretched over a sieve, while she did her cross-stitch and made a sassafras drink for the men and talked about the happy times before the monsters came.

"We used to go to Broadstairs for the summer. You ever been to the seaside, Dakin?" He shook his head. "Eh, poor little feller, fancy that! Deary me! Sometimes I wonder what we ever done to deserve having these monsters sent here."

"Your reckon they was sent, Mrs. Churt?"

"Oh, they were sent all right. I did hear, in the old days, factories used to dump all their rubbish in a quarry or out to sea; or, later on, up in the high sky, where they reckoned it'd blow away. Maybe somebody did the same thing with this little lot; just dumped them on us like kittens in a rain barrel. Or, maybe it was done out of spite; somebody had it in for us."

Corporal Bigtoe and a couple of privates came in asking if there was any chance of a hot drink. While Mrs. Churt served them, Dakin pondered over what she had suggested.

Could somebody have wanted to get rid of the monsters and just thought this was the best place to tip them?

Maybe there was something in what Mrs. Churt had said.

On the eighteenth day of travel they approached the outskirts of Manchester. Progress had been extremely slow for the last forty-eight hours. Several bridges had needed a lot of repair; and two of the men engaged on this work had been lost: Private Goodwillie was carried off by a Manticore, while Private Skulk had the misfortune to look at a Basilisk and of course died instantly.

"Didn't keep his Snark glasses properly greased," grumbled Sergeant Bellswinger.

"Snark glasses won't help, not against a Basilisk," said Corporal Enticknap. "In fact, if you ask me, Snark glasses aren't much good at all. What we need is a Snark mask, like what Driver Catchpole got issued."

"If you know so much, why don't you go to the colonel and say so?"

"I've a good mind to do just that."

"You go billocking to the colonel, I'll put you on wind-vane duty," growled the sergeant.

Wind-vane duty was very risky. It meant crawling along the top of the train, often through driving snow, clearing out the vanes, which soon became choked with dust when the train was in motion, and wiping the stellar energy panels. The worst danger was from Flying Hammerheads, but also the train rolled from side to side as it travelled, so there was a fair chance of being flung off.

Enticknap scowled, but remained silent. But when Dakin took in the colonel's beautifully polished boots next morning, the latter demanded, "What's all this about Snark masks?"

"They're saying as how the men ought to be issued with them, sir."

"Do you know how much a Snark mask costs, boy?" rapped the colonel.

"No, sir."

"Lord Ealing told me I was only to use them in the last resort."

"Where would the last resort be, sir?"

"Oh, go away!"

"Sir," said Dakin.

"Well? Now what?"

"Sir, I never get a chance to play my drum. Ser'nt Bellswinger won't let me. He says it makes too much finical row, that it would rouse up all the finical monsters between here and Gretna Green. Sir, when *can* I play it?"

"Don't you worry," said the colonel, rolling over under the velvet bedspread to help himself to another cup of tea. "You'll get to play it soon enough."

At that moment both Dakin and Colonel Clipspeak were greatly astonished to hear a voice apparently coming out of the colonel's early-morning teakettle. It said, "Hey, we gotta bloke here wants to get to Hempfields. What's it like out that way?"

"No go," said another voice. "It's a regular breeding ground for Snarks. Tell 'im, if 'e goes, it's at 'is own risk. The corporation won't admit liability."

"OK, I'll tell him that."

"You got Snarks your way too?"

"*Have* we got Snarks! Like starlings. Warrens full of 'em."

"They do say the young ones are harmless. You look at 'em, you don't vanish."

"You ever tried?"

"No, but my cousin Albert did. His kid brought one in for a pet. Cuddly little thing, it was."

"What happened?"

"It grew a bit older and looked at them and they all vanished."

"Well, then."

"What I mean is, if we could go after 'em when they're young . . ."

The two voices died away in a forest of crackle.

"Well, I'm blessed," said the colonel. "My kettle seems to have picked up a radio frequency."

"Yes, sir," said Dakin. "Hempfields is a place in Manchester, sir. My Auntie Floss used to live there. Do you think I might get to see my Auntie Floss by Christmas, sir? Aunt Floss used to have a tea-maker set like yours, sir."

"So did lots of people," snapped the colonel. "You send Major Scanty to me right away."

"Yessir."

"Come in, Scanty, come in," said the colonel, ten minutes later. "Help yourself to a glass of ginger wine. It was you, was it not, who received the radio message two days ago from Manchester?"

"Yes, Colonel."

"How did they contrive to send the message? I thought Manchester was deprived of all basic services."

"The mayor said—if I understood him correctly—that the vibrations set up by the wings of huge flocks of Snarks overhead created such exceptional static in the atmosphere that large portions of the city were infiltrated by electric current—even toothbrushes, carving knives, and hedge clippers became capable of transmitting electric messages—"

"Hmn, I see; like this kettle of mine. It just caught a chat between two radio cabs."

"Indeed sir. That kettle will be a decided asset if it continues to pick up external transmissions. Perhaps by means of it we shall be able to discover something about the causes and origins of the problems that we face," said Major Scanty hopefully.

The outskirts of Manchester were more devastated than those of London, in a different way. There were great greasy frozen swamps, with derelict factories, twisted metal girders, ruined concrete overpasses, and piles of snowy black coal-dust grown over with bindweed. But the town had not been flattened; far away in the distance highrise buildings could still be seen. The problem here had been Snarks, not the Shovel-tuskers which had knocked London flat.

Before it reached the city, the rail track sank down out of sight into a greenish peaty bog puddled all over with ice and rainbow patches of oil. A party of ten sappers was sent out to make good the track, layering it underneath with rapid-setting filler and plastic ties. The men wore well-greased Snark glasses and carried Kelpie knives for close combat; they were protected by another party in the driver's cab armed with flame-throwers and also December guns which fired explosive missiles of ice cooled to minus sixty degrees Celsius.

But despite this the work-party suffered badly. Dakin, dashing about in the cab, feverishly cleaning the big glass windows, wiping off Snark scales, Telepod fur, powder burns, and men's sweat, keeping the vision clear for the marksmen, was horrified to see how, man by man, the brave sappers were picked off. Six of them just vanished, when Snarks came too close, one was dragged away by a Telepod, one chopped in two by a Manticore and two were pulled into the swamp by Cocodrills. Just the same, in four days the task was finished. The track had been made usable and the *Cockatrice Belle* clanked slowly and cautiously over the doubtful stretch, and then very much faster up the slope beyond, Lance-Corporal Pitkin switching in half a dozen of his wind generators.

But the colonel was cursing long and bitterly as he paced about his cabin, with Major Scanty and Captain Twilight taking turns to look through the periscope that allowed a farther view of the track ahead.

"Some of my very best men! Those butterheads at supply just don't know the first thing about Snarks."

"How many real Snark masks were we given, sir?" asked Captain Twilight.

"Only enough for half the troop! And it's plain we're going to have a pitched battle on our hands before we can get into Manchester. The men will *have* to wear masks for that. Ensign Catchpole!" he barked over the intercom.

"Sir!"

"Cut your engine. We'll stop here for the night and recharge. Sergeant Bellswinger!"

"Yessir."

"We'll have a sally at first light tomorrow. Eighty men with full battle equipment—masks, Griffin capes, the lot. Meanwhile, tell the lads to take it easy and turn in early. And—harrumph—tell Mrs. Churt to give them something extra tasty for their evening meal. And, Bellswinger, send Drummer-boy Prestwich along here, will you?"

"Yessir."

Dakin was feeling depressed. He had seen ten people he knew, men who had been kind to him, cracked jokes, given him butter tokens, shown him a fast way to load his pistol, told him tales of Cockatrices, and how to deal with Bonnacons—he had seen those men vanish like drops of water on a hotplate and it had upset him badly. His expression was very dejected as he knocked and entered the colonel's cabin.

"Now, Prestwich," said the colonel, taking no notice of this, "there's a kind of monster in these parts that's hypersensitive to loud rhythmic noise."

"Sir?"

"The monsters can't stand a regular row. All the ones in the Apocarpus family are like that."

"I don't know no Apocarpuses, sir."

"We don't have many round London. But here there are whole schools of them. Hydra, Cocodrill, Glyptodont, Telepod, Kelpies, Griffins—they all belong to the Apocarpus family."

"Quite a big family, sir."

"If they hear a loud, sustained regular noise they tend to fall in half."

"Coo, sir."

"So you'll be out there tomorrow, with those eighty men, Prestwich, and I want you playing your drum really loud, so long as the battle lasts. D'you understand? I don't want you to stop for a single moment. Can you do that?"

"Coo, sir, yes sir!" said Dakin joyfully.

"Ask Mrs. Churt to give you a mug of hot milk with malt and molasses and rum flavouring in it, last thing tonight and first thing tomorrow. Tell her I said so."

"Yes, sir. Goodnight, sir!"

"Goodnight, Dakin."

"That ain't a bad boy," said Captain Twilight, as the brass-handled door closed behind Dakin. "He's got some sand in him."

When Dakin went along to Mrs. Churt for his bedtime drink, he found her with a melancholy, distant look in her eye. She too had been grieved by the loss of the ten men. But she was working even harder than usual at her cross-stitch canvas (it had a picture of a stylized Cockatrice on it, transfixed by a crossbow quarrel). A lot of the men had somehow acquired the notion that Mrs. Churt's piece of handiwork was a lucky charm, and many of them came seriously to touch it with one finger before retiring to bed.

"It's like the bit of turf in the centre of the Manchester United football pitch," said Private Tomkins. "Dead lucky, *that* is. You touch that with your finger, they say, you get all the good luck of everybody who ever stepped on it."

But Mrs. Churt was not paying attention. She sighed.

"That Corporal Bigtoe, he was a real one for a laugh. Come to that, they was all nice boys. Lively. I'd like to set up some kind of memorial to them."

"What kind, Mrs. Churt?" asked Dakin, sipping his hot molasses and milk.

"I'll have to think. Now, you hop it, off to bed. You got to keep busy, tomorrow."

Next day at dawn Dakin, reporting to the galley for his morning toddy, was surprised not to find Mrs. Churt presiding over the big copper cooking plates that were heated by power from the engine. Instead, Orderly Widgery was back in charge, stirring the cauldrons of porridge and toasting raisin buns for the men's breakfast.

"Where's Mrs. Churt?"

"Having a lie-in, I daresay, after that beanfeast she cooked last night."

Dakin thought this most unlike Mrs. Churt, but he had no time for more talk, the call for assembly was sounding on Catchpole's whistle; men were tumbling out of the big doors at the rear of the train, and forming into squares of ten. Dakin, who had been polishing his drum since 3:00 A.M., tumbled himself out likewise and took his place at the side of the troop, who all looked like unicorns in their pronged Snark masks. They carried long wicked December guns, squat, wide flame-throwers, and had Kelpie knives slotted all over their equipment wherever there was room.

"Now then—you little smitchy-faced article!" roared Sergeant Bellswinger to Dakin. "You keep your eye on Captain Twilight there, and follow wherever he goes. When I say the word *march*, you begins to play, and you doesn't stop till you hears Catchpole sound the recall. Understand? Comprenny? Troop! Shun! Verse—arms! Eyes—front! Left—turrrn! At the double—MARRCH!"

"Titherump, titherump, titherump, rat-a-tat-tat-tat-tat-tat-*tum!*" sang Dakin's drum under his rattling drumsticks, as he panted along in Captain Twilight's rear beside the troop of men, who were hurrying grimly and gaily up towards the top of a long rough slope of moorland. When they reached the summit they could see down on the other side, through the morning mist, the battered tower blocks of Manchester.

Between the troop and the town, though, swarmed a wild medley of monsters, hopping, swooping, galloping on nine legs, gliding on slimy suckers, prancing on claw-fringed hoofs, floating on bat-wings.

"Croopus," said Private Mollisk. " 'Tis like 'The Teddy Bears' Picnic'."

"As good as a panto," said Private Reilly. "All we need's the Fairy Queen."

"Rumpa-tumpa, tumpa, tump!" beat Dakin's drumsticks.

"Squad-load!" bawled Sergeant Bellswinger. "On the word—*fire!*"

A sheet of flame and a black hail of missiles swept across the open space.

It was a ferocious battle. Out of the mists to the south a dim red sun presently mounted and cast patches of crimson light on the frosty slope, on the grisly many-shaped monsters and the men, who looked almost as wild, in their Griffin capes, Gorgon shields, and Snark masks.

Dakin, too, had been issued with a Snark mask. It was much too big for him and kept slipping; every few minutes he had to hitch his head back to shake it into position. He longed to take it off and sling it over his shoulder, but he did not, for three reasons: first, Sergeant Bellswinger had threatened to cut his tripes out if he did so; second, he observed Ensign Crisworthy take *his* mask off to blow his nose and, a second later, vanish like a burnt tissue as a Snark winged down on him; third, rattling away at the big drum like a mad woodpecker, Dakin simply hadn't time to do anything but keep drumming.

Sometimes the fight roared and seethed all around him, sometimes it swept away into the distance; sometimes he had the satisfaction of seeing some beast pause, hesitate, catching the sound of his desperate tattoo, and then suddenly fall in half like a tree struck by lightning. On the whole he received very little notion as to how the general trend of the battle was going, whether the Cockatrice Corps might be winning or losing. There seemed to be an unlimited supply of monsters; they kept pouring out of the sky, and from the towers of Manchester, like swarming seagulls or hungry lo-

custs. Dakin thumped away, often ducking a whistling wing, or leaping aside to dodge a raking talon; once he was wrapped in slimy tentacles and had to slash himself loose at frantic speed with his Kelpie knife, transferring both drumsticks to his left hand temporarily; but not once did he stop drumming, not even when he thought he saw Mrs. Churt hurry across the hillside among the men in their dark-brown uniforms and the cream-coloured, salmon-pink, yellow, grey, and leopard-spotted monsters.

"I must have *imagined* that I saw Mrs. Churt," Dakin thought. "What on earth would she be doing in a scrimmage like this? Maybe I'm getting feverish. I've got cramps in my arms and feet, and I can't feel my hands at all."

Then, all of a sudden, the battle was over. Not because one side or the other had gained a definite victory, but simply because of the weather. Sharp, slashing javelins of snow hissed down out of the low grey clouds, now purpling towards sunset, the sunset of Christmas Eve; the snow cut and stung and blinded men and monsters alike. In five minutes hardly a living creature was to be seen on the rough hillside. Bodies lay scattered here and there—men, Manticores, Snarks, Hydras, Cocodrills, tossed higgledy-piggledy. Dakin recognized the bodies of two men and an officer, Captain Twilight, but he was too dead-tired to feel anything but a kind of puzzled sadness. His one wish was to find his way back to the train, fall on his bunk and sleep for a hundred hours. Had the recall been sounded? And which *was* the way back? During the battle he had been pushed further and further along the slope; now he found himself at the foot of a shallow gully, but it was hard to see more than a few yards through the slicing, stinging snow.

It must be right if I keep going downhill, he thought and ran, stumbling and slipping, as fast as he could over the tussocky ground, his drum banging awkwardly on his hip. A layer of snow caked over his Snark mask, blinding him, so he took off the mask. Snarks can't like this weather any more than I do, he decided. And if I keep it on I shall only walk into a river or something.

Looking everywhere for the troop train, he was dismayed to see instead a high wall ahead of him. It was so high that its top was veiled in cloud and snow. Oh crumbs, I must have gone wrong; that must be Manchester town wall. I'll just have to turn round and go back—

Before he could turn he was halted by a shout. "Who goes there? Man or monster? Stop or I shoot!"

"I'm a m-m-m-man," called Dakin through chattering teeth. His uniform was soaked through and his boots were full of snow; he felt like an icicle.

"Man? You don't look like it," said the voice. "Well, come forward—but slowly—for if either of us makes a mistake you'll end up with a stomach full of red-hot sand."

Dakin scrunched slowly over the snow towards a narrow gate which he now saw in the wall ahead of him.

"Holy smoke!" said the voice. "It *is* a nipper! Wait till the warden of the gate hears this. Come along in, you poor little sardine—you must be half perished."

Five minutes later Dakin found himself in a warm, bright, noisy place—the barrack-room of the Manchester town wall guard squad—where he was given a cup of hot herb tea, rubbed with towels, and questioned eagerly by the warden, the mayor, all the guards officers, and half the citizens of Manchester, about the battle, his part in it, and the cargo of the *Cockatrice Belle*.

"We did manage to set up radio transmissions, you see,

but then lost them again when that cloud of monsters swooped down so low," the mayor explained. "And the visibility was so bad, and the Snark glass in the town wall windows is so thick, that we couldn't see what was happening. Often enough, the monsters have battles among themselves; we couldn't be sure it wasn't that."

You might have sent a party out to *make* sure, Dakin thought, but he was too tactful to say so.

"We're all a bit weak here, you see," the mayor apologized. "Half a cup of thin gruel each a day for the last six weeks."

Dakin realized that the Manchester men did look desperately thin and pale; he forgave them for not dashing out to help their rescuers.

"There's a big load of tinned carrots on the train," he said.

"*Carrots!* I'll have a try at making radio contact again now that dark has fallen."

Radio contact was presently established from the mayor's electric shaver to Colonel Clipspeak's teakettle and Dakin learned that the men of the sally party had fought their way back to the train, having inflicted heavy casualties on the monsters and not suffered too badly themselves. The colonel was delighted to hear that his drummer boy was safe in Manchester, and promised to send in the carrot supply at first light as a Christmas present for the population of Manchester.

"The boy had better stay with you; we'll pick him up in the morning."

Dozens of people offered Dakin a bed for the night. He had never felt so popular. But he said, "My Auntie Floss used to live in Manchester. If she's still alive! Mrs. Florence Monsoon. And my cousin Sauna. I'd like to see them if they're still here."

Somebody knew where Mrs. Monsoon lived, in a highrise block called Brylcreme Court, and Dakin was taken there in the mayor's rickshaw, pulled by a dozen weak but grateful citizens.

Brylcreme Court was a gaunt concrete tower at the end of a cul-de-sac.

"The stairs are through that door," coughed the mayor's son, and pointed with a shaking hand. "You won't mind if we don't come up? Weeks of gruel don't leave your legs up to climbing stairs. Your auntie's at number fifteen."

Dakin said of course he could find his way, thanked them all heartily, and started up the steps. After weeks on the one-storey train and the long day's battle, his own legs did not feel any too strong.

As he toiled slowly up the concrete flights, illuminating his way by sparing flashes of his Hydra torch, a queer feeling took hold of him. What was it? In the battle he'd had no time to feel frightened; the monsters did not scare him. But now he realized that the hungry, shadowy feeling inside him was fear. He was afraid, and yet he did not know why.

As he neared the door of number fifteen he found himself walking more and more slowly.

The door, which was shabby, dirty, and battered, had a little spy hole in it. When Dakin stood outside, his heart went pit-a-pat. He heard people talking in the flat.

"I can see Cousin Dakin," said a soft voice, and a louder, sharper voice said, "Oh, don't be such a pest, Sauna. You put me quite out of patience, that you do."

Then there came the sound of a brisk slap and a low cry.

Dakin tapped on the door.

Immediately there was complete silence inside. Then a pale-grey eye surveyed him through the spy hole.

"Who's that?" snapped a voice—the same that had said, "You put me out of patience."

"Drummer Dakin Prestwich looking for his auntie, Mrs. Monsoon."

The door opened slowly. A skinny woman stood regarding him with suspicion. Then her face cleared a little.

"Well—upon my word. It *is* Dakin. Whatever are you doing here?"

"Come to give you Mum's best wishes," said Dakin. "I was on the troop train that brought the carrots to Manchester."

"Oh! *Carrots!*" breathed the girl who stood behind Mrs. Monsoon. She was Dakin's size, or a little taller, red-haired, and would have been nice-looking if she were not so thin and sad.

"Cousin Sauna!" Dakin exclaimed. "Remember how you used to play my mouth-organ?"

He would have shaken hands with her, but strangely enough Sauna's hands were tied behind her with a strip of rag.

"We have to do that," hastily explained her aunt, observing Dakin's look of puzzled outrage. "Sauna's too active for this flat. She'd have everything topsy-turvy in no time."

There was not an inch of spare space in Mrs. Monsoon's tiny apartment, Dakin noticed. Hundreds of little china pots covered every surface.

"It was my hobby. Used to collect 'em. Brought 'em back as souvenirs from holidays," said Aunt Floss, noticing Dakin's eyes on the pots. "Then Sauna's mum and dad died abroad and I had to bring *her* back. And then, of course, we had to stop travelling." It was plain that she blamed her niece for this.

Dakin began to feel very sorry for Sauna, shut up in such a small place with all those pots, as well as Florence Monsoon, who looked to him like a short-tempered woman. The basement of Barclays Bank, Shepherd's Bush, was a paradise in comparison.

"Well, Dakin," Mrs. Monsoon said sharply, confirming

his impression of her, "you can't stop the night here, for we've no room, as you can see. Maybe Mrs. Beadnik, who moved in across the way, could take you; I'll just step across and ask her. Don't you touch nothing while I'm gone."

The moment she was out of the door, Dakin cut through the rag fastening Sauna's wrist with his Kelpie knife.

"How *can* she tie you up like that?" he said. "It's dreadful!"

"Oh, no, it's really best," Sauna told him earnestly. "Otherwise I'm sure to knock something over. She only ties my hands during the day . . . But, Dakin, I don't think it's a good plan your going to stay with Mrs. Beadnik—she's not very nice, she's rather queer. She only came to this building a few weeks ago."

"Maybe I'd better go back to the barracks," said Dakin doubtfully.

But Sauna's eyes suddenly grew large as saucers and she gazed at Dakin in fright.

"Oh, Dakin! I can see a woman who knows you! She's out in the street, being chased by a Manticore!"

"How do you mean, you see her?"

"She's in the street down below. Her name's Mrs. Churt."

"But *how* can you see her?" demanded Dakin, for the windows had thick blinds over them.

"Oh, I can see through walls. Quick, quick, let's go and help her!"

As they scampered down the steep concrete stairs Dakin panted, "Will Aunt Floss be very angry when she finds you've gone out?"

"Oh, no, I'm sure not. She's very fed up with me. She often says she wishes she'd never had to take charge of me. Look! look there . . ."

Sauna had pulled Dakin round a couple of street corners, running through the dark, silent town. Now they came to a bit of a waste land covered with lavender bushes—the scent was very strong—and they saw Mrs. Churt being chased by a huge Manticore. She was running clumsily, weighed down by the two heavy baskets she carried. The beast was gaining on her at every bound, it was just about to pounce—

"Stop it, stop it!" screamed Sauna.

Dakin dragged out his liquid-air pistol, aimed it as best he could with shaking hands, and pressed down the plunger. A fierce narrow jet, unbelievably much colder than ice, melted the Manticore into dark-blue jelly when it was only two leaps behind Mrs. Churt.

"Well, my gracious!" exclaimed that lady. "I *am* pleased to see you, young Dakin! I thought I was a goner that time! Wish we could make him into blackberry tart," she added, looking critically at the dissolved monster. "And who's this little beauty, eh?"

"This is my cousin Sauna," said Dakin, thinking how much better his cousin looked when her cheeks were pink with excitement.

"Pleased to meet you dearie. I can see you're a gal as'll go far—in fact I been dreaming about you, my love, these last two to three nights; I thought we'd be meeting soon! Now we'd best be getting back to the train. I'd have been back long ago, making sorrel soup for the lads, if that monster hadn't chased me out of my way." And Mrs. Churt indicated her baskets laden with winter spinach and greenery. "I got a little bit of white heather too, to grow in a pot as a memorial for Corporal Bigtoe and those others what got killed."

"But how *can* we get back to the train, Mrs. Churt? We're inside the town wall."

"Yes, dear, but there's a way through here no one seems to have noticed, prob'ly because it's all covered by them lavender bushes."

And nipping along with great confidence as if crossing her own back garden Mrs. Churt led them along a narrow gully, back to where the *Cockatrice Belle* was parked. It was lit from end to end, as the combatants sang and drank sassafras tea with rum in it, and played table tennis, and discussed the battle, and planned next day's manoeuvres. All the red and green Christmas bells were being rung by an invention of Corporal Widgery, from heat generated by the men as they played ping-pong.

Colonel Clipspeak was pleased to see Dakin back, and even happier to welcome Mrs. Churt, who had been given up for lost.

"Never, *ever* leave the train again without an escort," he scolded her. "We can't spare you, Mrs. Churt!"

"No, but you'll be glad of all these lovely greens I got," she replied placidly. "A beautiful mess o' salad I'll be able to make for the boys now. And this young lady's going to come and be my helper, aren't you, dear?"

"That young person? Certainly not!" exclaimed the colonel. "One female on this train is quite enough. Two would be entirely out of the question."

"Oh, now, sir, don't be hasty, just you wait! Don't you go for to be so sticklish! This young lady's got a real talent, haven't you, dearie?" said Mrs. Churt comfortably. "She can see things as hasn't happened yet—through walls and all, she can see 'em."

It took a long time, and a lot of argument, to convince the colonel that Sauna would be a really useful member of the crew on board the *Cockatrice Belle*. That night she had to demonstrate again and again that she really could see things—Hammerheads, Cockatrices, and people—not only through walls, but sometimes ten minutes before they arrived, or even earlier.

At last the colonel said, "Oh, very well! She may come for a trial trip. Just on the run back to London. I don't promise more than that! Should a message be sent to her family apprising them of my decision?"

Accordingly, next morning, Christmas Day, while the carrots were being delivered under guard, a note was despatched to Auntie Floss requesting the services of Miss Sauna Blow as Assistant Mess Orderly (Female) Supernumerary Second Grade on the *Cockatrice Belle*.

But, strangely enough, Aunt Floss was not to be found among her thousands of small china souvenirs. Nor, by her neighbours, was she ever seen again. Her new neighbour Mrs. Beadnik seemed to have vanished at the same time.

But the disappearance of people was such a commonplace that no one thought much about it.

Only several days later did Sauna, stirring soup in the galley, suddenly exclaim, "Oh! My goodness!"

"What is it, dearie?" enquired Mrs. Churt, chopping raisins. "Don't let that soup boil over, lovey; shift it to one side."

"Oh, it was just I remembered the baby Snark I found that last evening, sheltering by the dustbins, when I threw out the tea leaves. (Chopped grass they were, really, but Aunt Floss used them for telling futures.) The baby Snark looked so miserable and floppy I thought I'd bring it in for a warm-up. So I put it in the airing cupboard, and I was going to let it out first thing on Christmas morning before Aunt Floss came across it. Only I forgot. Now I do wonder . . ."

"Well, let that be a lesson to you, dearie," said Mrs. Churt. "Your auntie don't sound no great loss from all that I heard. But there's some things as oughtn't to be brought inside. And we certainly don't want no baby Snarks on *this* train."

Chapter three

For various reasons, it was just as well that Sauna's first few days aboard the *Cockatrice Belle* were passed in the shelter of Manchester's underground railway station, to which roomy, if gloomy, refuge the train had been shifted under cover of dark.

"Why don't the train start off and *go* somewhere?" asked Sauna, puzzled and a touch dissatisfied, on the first morning. "I thought trains was supposed to go swizzing all over the country?"

"We're waiting for orders," Dakin explained. "The *Belle*'s an army train, see. We got to get a message from the commander-in-chief up in London town afore we can take off."

"Who's he?"

"General Grugg-Pennington."

"So why the pize don't he send off an order, 'stead of having the troops eating their heads off in Manchester?"

Sauna was extremely anxious to get away from that city. Although no further news or information had been received regarding Aunt Floss, the time spent by Sauna in her stuffy flat had been so shadowy and horrible that even a mention of it was enough to cast her into depression. And the possibility of ever going back there was not to be thought of.

"What did she do that was so awful?" Dakin asked once.

"I don't want to talk about her. And," said Sauna, "I don't believe the baby Snark did do for her. She'd soon send it packing. Anyway," she asked, "why don't General Grugg-Thingummy send the colonel an order, then?"

"Colonel Clipspeak can't get through to London. There's too much cosmic dust interference over London."

Despite Sauna's wish to get away, this had certain advantages. Just at present there was so much stored-up energy inside her, after years spent in her aunt's tiny flat with hands tied behind her back, that she might have found the cramped quarters allotted to Assistant mess Orderly (Female) on the *Cockatrice Belle* no great improvement. But while the train was at a standstill military rules were somewhat relaxed. The troops could play table tennis and snooker on platform one, while Sauna and Dakin were permitted to race up and down platform two hundreds of times a day, until a bit of Sauna's pent-up force had been dissipated.

"Bless her liddle heart, I only wish we could send her out on useful errands for wild garlic roots and samphire," remarked Mrs. Churt, glancing out of the window as she brought in Colonel Clipspeak's mid-morning oatmeal muffin and cup of acorn coffee. "Look at them, how they do scamper! It's a shame they can't go outside, but I can see that wouldn't do, not with all these boojums and Telepods a-fluttering around."

Then Colonel Clipspeak had a practical idea.

"Issue the gal with a skipping-rope," he told Sergeant Bellswinger.

"A skipping-rope, sir?" The sergeant was taken aback. "I don't reckon as there's such an article on board, Colonel, sir."

"Well! Use your ingenuity, dammit, man! Make one! Find something in the stores that can be converted."

So a piece of cord was unwound from around a crate of Gorgon goggles, and handles were contrived from some as yet unused Hydra truncheons.

"There you are, chick," said Handyman-Corporal Nark, presenting Sauna with the finished article.

"What's it for? What do I do with it?" demanded Sauna, gazing in bemusement at the length of rope with a handle at each end.

"You never used a skip-rope, you poor little commodity? Why, you skips with it. You does it like this. Come on to the platform."

He was about to demonstrate, when Sergeant Bellswinger ordered. "Here! You pass that to me. *I'll* show her."

Tall, stringy, bony and red-faced, the sergeant had not manipulated a skipping-rope in over forty years. But the skill with which he had been accustomed to outskip his sister Lil on Stepney Green had not deserted him: he could perform on his right foot or his left, or both, double-through, pirouette, and even achieve two cuts-up and a polka, meanwhile whistling Suppé's *Light Cavalry* overture. Sauna watched completely absorbed.

"Coo!" she breathed. "It'll take me years and *years* to do it as good as you, Ser'nt!"

"Wants plenty o' practice, that's all," said the sergeant, puffing modestly, handing back the rope. "Maybe, once we're in motion, the colonel might give permission for you to use the observation platform."

In the meantime, all day and every day, Sauna practised on platform two, and in less than forty-eight hours fifty more hand-crafted skipping-ropes had made their appearance up and down the train; and half the Cockatrice Corps were out practising along with her.

"Not very dignified, hey, Sergeant?" said the colonel.

"Never mind, sir, it'll do 'em no harm. Keeps 'em fit, and their mind off things," said the sergeant. "Just till you gets that-ere message."

For the cosmic interference between London and Manchester had increased to such a degree that as yet no orders had come through from headquarters.

But one morning Sauna carried the colonel's breakfast plateful of bread and butter to this cabin. (He continued to prefer brewing his own tea with the electric kettle, for he said Mrs. Churt's tea was like doormat clippings soaked in Worcestershire Sauce; but he did enjoy a piece of her fresh-baked carrot bread, thinly sliced and buttered, with his tea.)

Sauna, laying the bone-china plate with its two paper-fine slices on the mahogany bedside shelf, suddenly cried out: "Oh, mercy me, sir, why your kettle's a-talking to you—just like the one in my Auntie Floss's place, that is . . . Well I never!"

"I heard nothing?" said the colonel snappishly. (Sauna had woken him from an enjoyable dream of winning the regimental point-to-point on his grey charger Battleaxe, long since, alas, rendered down into soup and Snark masks.) "What, pray, child, did you understand the kettle to say?"

"It said—half a mo, now, it's talking again—it's a-saying *Leicester Square Command Post*, Gladiolus, Gladiolus. Five two zero six three."

"Indeed?"

"*Cockatrice Belle, Cockatrice Belle,*" went on Sauna. "Proceed south to Willoughby-on-the-Wolds via Lincoln, where you will pick up the Archbishop, Dr. Philip Wren."

"Good heavens. Go on. Via Lincoln, you said?"

"At Willoughby-on-the-Wolds take on board consignment of special-trained German Gridelin hounds. Then reroute in a northerly direction, destination approximate locality of the Kingdom of Fife. More briefing for this mission will be supplied later. Do you receive me? Gladiolus, Gladiolus, over, over and out. Message ends."

"God bless my soul!" bellowed the colonel, shooting upright in bed and staring at Sauna. His eyeglass fell out into the bread and butter.

"Can you repeat that?" he enquired more quietly in a minute, picking up one of the slices of bread and butter, removing his eyeglass from it, folding the slice into four, and demolishing it in one snap.

"Oh yes, sir," Sauna said. "I'm ever so good at learning by heart. Because of all the time I was tied up at Auntie's. I used to learn the phone book, for that's all there was."

And she repeated the message to the colonel twice more.

"What was it saying at the start, when you first heard it?" demanded the colonel, beginning on his second slice of carrot bread.

"Only the date," said Sauna. "New Year's Day."

"But that isn't today," objected the colonel. "That's the day after tomorrow."

"Oh, I often gets a message two days ahead," explained Sauna. "Auntie used to get real cross and upset, for I'd see the postman coming up the front steps on Monday, and then he wouldn't ring the bell till Wednesday."

"Humph," said the colonel. "Most remarkable. You can run along now, child. But send Major Scanty and Lieutenant Upfold to me."

By the time these officers had reached his walnut-panelled state-room the colonel was up and dressed and pacing about. He kept referring to a large relief map of the United Kingdom which occupied the whole of the end wall.

"Ahem, gentlemen! It seems that the child Sauna, as well as being able to see through walls, has also a proclivity of precognition. She can receive a message from GHQ forty-eight hours before it is sent."

"Quite convenient that, sir," remarked Lieutenant Upfold.

"Most gratifying," said Major Scanty.

"Too bad they ain't running the Derby these days," went on the lieutenant thoughtfully. "We'd all stand to make our fortunes."

The colonel quelled him with a frown.

"It appears probable," he continued, "that the day after tomorrow we shall receive instructions to proceed to Willoughby-on-the-Wolds, via Lincoln, and then direct our course northwards once more, towards the Kingdom of Fife in Scotland."

"Scotland! Bless my soul! We should see some lively action up there, I fancy. Chimeras and Chichivaches they have in those parts, do they not?"

"Lincoln," murmured the Lieutenant. "Pity it ain't the season for Lincoln races."

"The Kingdom of Fife, eh?" meditated Major Scanty. "I seem to recollect hearing about a great concentration of monsters in that region—as if some malign influence might be directing them from thereabouts. It has always been a queer cut-off region: the Firth of Forth below it, and the Firth of Tay above. And the Ochils to the west—those hills have always had a most sinister reputation. Six-legged beasts, you know, and queer things coming out of holes. Though I believe the Scots are not troubled by Snarks; the climate, fortunately, is too cold for them north of the Roman Wall."

Major Scanty was a thin, quiet, learned professor of zoology from Fishguard University who had been co-opted into the army because of his extensive knowledge of, and acquaintance with monsters.

"What they do have in Scotland and the north of England," he pursued, "is an abundance of Trolls and Kelpies. Trolls have become a large-scale pest. However, very fortunately, they are only active at night. Kelpies may be encountered at any time, but, on the whole, not beyond ten miles or so from the coast. (Or, of course, from lakes and rivers.) The impressions of their feet are to be found in the red sandstone of Forfarshire," he told his colleagues.

"Quite so! Quite so!" snapped the colonel. "No doubt we shall require different defences and methods of warfare against such beings from those required against monsters in the Midlands. That, however, can be discussed as we proceed on our way to Willoughby."

"Er?" enquired Lieutenant Upfold diffidently. "I suppose there is a station at Willoughby-on-the-Wolds?"

The colonel threw him another quelling look from under bushy white eyebrows and had recourse to the wall map again.

"Harrumph!" he remarked, after a few minutes' intensive study. "It seems that there is not. But there appear to be stations at Old Dalby and Nether and Upper Broughton, not too far distant from Willoughby. No doubt an expeditionary force may be despatched from one of those. I ask myself *why*, of all locations in the kingdom, that obscure spot should have been chosen for the delivery of those animals."

"What animals, sir?"

"Specially trained Gridelin hounds from Germany."

"Oh, gracious me, what a piece of good fortune!" exclaimed Major Scanty, his thin face alight with enthusiasm. "I have heard of those, yes, indeed I have! And always wished to make a study of them. I understand that they are *sovereign* in use against Telepods and Bycorns; also against that much more dangerous beast, the Mirkindole."

"Don't know Mirkindoles," remarked Lieutenant Upfold, studying the map. "Are they a northern special, like Trolls and Kelpies?"

"Yes, indeed they are. The Mirkindole, you may know, a member of the Basilisk family, has a tiger's body and the face of an elderly dyspeptic gentleman with long curling horns. It is particularly deadly, since the eyes have hypnotic power. But the Gridelin hounds, I have heard, are champions at running them down. What a superlatively lucky circumstance that we are to be equipped with some of these excellent and faithful canine quadrupeds. I believe I have heard that they are bred in Hanover. From where, I wonder, and from whom have they been sent?"

"No idea at present," said the colonel. "The message didn't state. Now here's a knotty question, and I'd like your views on it, gentlemen."

The two officers looked at him attentively.

"The message, which the child Sauna passed to me, was dated New Year's Day, two days ahead of where we are now. Ought I to act upon it immediately? Set out directly? Or—or not?"

As the colonel put this question an extremely loud crash

was heard overhead, and a few pieces of broken metal and glass were seen to fall past the windows on to the station platform. (Fortunately it happened to be the period of the crew's mid-morning snack-break, and all the men, as well as Sauna and Dakin, were aboard the train, partaking of watery cocoa and turnip crackers.)

"Bellswinger!" barked the colonel on the intercom. "What was that?"

"It was a dive-bomb attack by half a dozen Snarks, sir," came Bellswinger's reply. "On the station roof at ground level. But they done themselves in, not one of 'em survived. We got all the bodies, and I've a party of men up there already, sir, repairing the hole with brown paper and filler-tape."

"Tape! That won't hold them off for long, man."

"I know, sir, but it's all we got left. Stores are running low."

"Humph! Very well, Thanks, Sergeant."

The colonel replaced the receiver of his house-phone. "I think that settles it, gentlemen. We can't afford to remain here any longer. To keep on the move is our only hope of survival. And we can pick up some more stores at Lincoln."

"But can you get a message through to Leicester Square command post?" asked the major doubtfully. "To tell them your plans?"

"That is what we now have to discover. Upfold, pray fill the kettle and switch it on."

The kettle, though convenient, was a chancy and unreliable instrument for transmitting and receiving messages. Sometimes, when boiling briskly, it would render loud and clear conversations between people or stations who were many thousands of miles apart.

"South Pole, South Pole to Command Station Tasmania: we are running out of herrings. Over."

"Easter Island here, South Pole. I think we have a crossed line. No herrings in this area. Only heads. Over . . ."

"Capricorn-Cancer Area Control speaking. We have no herrings. Could let you have a few goats or crabs . . ."

"Perhaps the kettle might perform better if the child Sauna were present in the room?" diffidently suggested Lieutenant Upfold. "As a small radio, you know, often works better if somebody is holding it?"

"Possibly so, possibly," snapped the colonel, vexed that he had not thought of this himself. "Bellswinger!" he ordered on the intercom. "Let the child Sauna be sent here at once. On the double."

Sauna arrived on the double, out of breath, and with smudges of black on her face and the pillow-ticking apron she wore over her army issue dungarees. (During her sojourn on the *Cockatrice Belle*, brief as it had been, she had already grown out of the tattered clothes which had been big enough while she was surviving on a siege diet.)

"Sir!" she panted, saluting smartly as Bellswinger had taught her.

"Why is your face black, child?"

"Polishing buttons, sir."

"Oh, very well. Never mind it. Pray lay your hand over the handle of that kettle."

"Yessir . . ."

At the end of two hours all the persons in the colonel's cabin were red-faced, wild-haired, and damp with perspiration. The room was full of steam. But a tolerably workable method had been evolved, by means of which, with Upfold using the colonel's dress sabre as an aerial, holding its tip against the spout of the kettle and pointing the hilt in variations of three hundred and sixty degrees, contact with the Leicester Square headquarters was at last established.

Not before some very odd conjunctions, however.

A stream of spiky language issuing from the spout of the kettle threw Major Scanty into transports of excitement, and was identified by him as Hungarian. It seemed he had once spent time in that country and had friends there. Indeed he would have liked to prolong the conversation.

"They tell me, colonel, that there are no monsters at all in their country; indeed the continent of Europe is at present free from such a plague as has infested this kingdom. Is not that very singular, sir?"

"It would be if it were so, but I don't for a moment believe it," grunted the colonel, who wanted his lunch. "Why should this island be singled out for special misusage? A most improbable notion! Pray, Upfold, shift the blade and try to find us the correct station."

Upfold, frowning with the concentration required to shift the sword blade the infinitesimal fraction of a centimetre that would pick up a different wavelength, obeyed and a pale-blue flame ran, for a second, along the sabre to the kettle.

A tiny, distant, but crystal-clear voice commanded: "*Unloose the tempest.*"

"*Master. It shall be done.*"

"*Find the loose connection. Destroy it.*"

"*To hear is to obey.*"

Lieutenant Upfold's concentration slipped momentarily and a new voice took over.

"Saturn, Saturn," it was saying impatiently. "Ring five hundred and two. Five hundred and two. Please adjust your circumference. Adjust your circumference. We have crackle from cosmic dust."

Pressing his lips together, knuckles white with strain, Upfold at last found the correct point in the invisible dome of air above the kettle, and stood like a statue while Colonel Clipspeak enjoyed a brisk, businesslike conversation with General Grugg-Pennington, who happened at that very time to be holding a conference with Lord Ealing in Leicester Square tube station.

"Sir, is it true that you are arranging for despatch of Gridelin hounds to Willoughby-on-the-Wolds?"

"Now, how in the world did you know that?" said the general, utterly astonished. "Why, yes—I have the intention of doing so, but how you can have received news of the plan I can't imagine, for the beasts have not yet embarked. They come from Hanover and are to be sent by submarine from Amsterdam and by canal boat from Harwich to Willoughby. The journey should take two days. But the risks are severe, and the chances of their safe arrival are not encouraging. I do not like this *at all*, Clipspeak. By what means did you get wind of our intentions? Can there be a leak in our security?"

"Pray don't be concerned, General. There is no leak, I believe I can assure you. It is just that by remarkable good fortune we rescued from Manchester a young person who has unusual telepathic and precognitive dexterity. Indeed, it is only because of this that I am able to talk to you know."

"Oh, very well. If you say so. But now, listen, Clipspeak, in case we have more trouble making contact. I want you to take the *Belle* on to Scotland. It appears that this whole evil invasion of our island is being directed from somewhere in that locality. The rest of Europe is clear, so far."

"Oh, indeed, sir, how singular. That is in fact what Scanty—but I—"

"Don't interrupt, Clipspeak. It is being directed from a command post in Scotland. We have been given two possible names: Crook of Devon and Rumbling Bridge. Your mission is to discover this post and destroy it. So after Willoughby and the acquisition of the hounds, proceed northwards."

"Who is—?"

"Who? We don't know. Nor why. But our intelligence is positive that orders are being issued from somewhere in the triangle between Crook of Devon, Rumbling Bridge, and the town of Dollar."

"Is there a railway station at one of those places?" Colonel Clipspeak asked doubtfully.

"That is for you to ascertain! Possibly the nearest rail point may be Gleneagles—"

"Thank you, sir."

"Do not fail us, Clipspeak! The safety of the kingdom may rest with you. Indeed, that of all Europe! The plague may spread. You must set out at once. Do not forget to pick up the Archbishop, who will be expecting you."

"Yes, sir," said Clipspeak faintly.

"Over and out."

Colonel Clipspeak mopped his brow with his stiff white pipe-clayed gloves. Sauna quietly prised the lid off and peered inside the kettle.

"Could you switch off?" she whispered to the lieutenant. "It's just a-going to boil dry."

Thankfully laying down the heavy sabre, Upfold switched off the kettle at the wall plug.

Major Scanty was trembling with excitement.

"Then what those chaps in Hungary told us is true!" he exclaimed. "The main part of Europe has not been troubled by this plague of monsters. It is only our own kingdom which has been so afflicted. Now why, I ask myself, should that be?"

"I can think of plenty of likely reasons why," muttered the lieutenant. But Colonel Clipspeak had bent on Sauna his piercing dark eyes, all the more brilliant for being set deep under bristly thickets of white eyebrow.

"Now then, miss! It's high time we knew more about *you.* All we know is that Dakin the drummer rescued you from this siege city. And that you are his cousin."

"Yessir, my mam and his mam were sisters. But my mam and dad died, you see, and I've been looked arter by my Auntie Floss."

"How did your parents die, child?"

"In a plane crash, sir. We was all going together for a holiday in Marbella, when the plane engine conked out."

"And your parents were killed?"

"Yessir," faltered Sauna, wiping away a couple of tears with a corner of her apron.

"And you? How was it that you did not die also?"

"I'd put on my life jacket, sir, like they told us, and the strap caught in a fig tree as I fell. And, by and by, some Spanish chaps lifted me down. And the next thing I knew, my Auntie Floss Monsoon had come to Spain to fetch me home. A'cos Mam and Dad were dead."

"Their names were?"

"Ted and Emily Blow, sir. Dad used to be a chimney sweep in Newcastle, sir. That was where we lived."

"So then you went to live in Manchester with your aunt. Had you known her before?"

"No, sir, never. Mam nor Dad never spoke of her, but she told me she was a cousin of my da."

"Was she kind to you?"

"She was strict," said Sauna, after some thought. "It was

having my hands tied all the blessed time that was the worst."

"And this gift of yours—being able to see and hear events and information before they have come to pass—have you had that always?"

"Oh no, sir," said Sauna simply. "Only since the plane crashed, and Mam and Dad died, and I hung for six hours in that-there fig tree."

"And did your aunt know of your gift?"

"Yes, sir. She didn't like it."

"I see. Thank you child. Ahem. You may return to your duties."

"It is the most remarkable piece of luck that we should have happened to take her on board," said Colonel Clipspeak, when Sauna had slipped thankfully away to her button polishing.

"I wonder, though, was it pure luck?" mused Major Scanty. "Or was it preordained?"

"What can you mean?" demanded the colonel.

"Did you hear, sir, that singular little passage before Upfold here found the correct frequency for command headquarters?"

"All that idiocy about crabs and goats and herrings? Sounded like balderdash to me."

"No, just the two brief exchanges about the tempest. And a loose connection."

"Can't say I paid it any heed," said the colonel.

"It make me think," said Major Scanty. He stopped and rubbed his chin, looking thoughtfully at the colonel, who was beginning to fill in a large form, muttering to himself, "If we are to take on board the Archbishop of Lincoln, we shall need to make certain that *all* the formalities are most duly and carefully observed."

But Lieutenant Upfold threw a keen glance at the major.

"You mean, sir, when that voice said 'Unloose the tempest!' And a blue flame ran down the sword blade? I must confess it sent a cold shiver down *my* spine."

"Oh, fiddle-de-dee!" snapped the colonel, hunting among all his pens for one that would write. "Why, if that was anything at all to the purpose, it was just some meteorological station giving a forecast. Probably in Japan. Much good that will do us."

"I fear you may be right," sighed the major.

But Lieutenant Upfold shook his head.

"Those voices were deuced queer, if you ask me. Gave me the shivering hab-dabs. There was something—" he searched for words—"something not at all *the thing* about those voices. Specially one of them. Not like anything I've ever heard in my life before. Nor," he added after some thought, "anything like what I'd ever want to hear again."

"Oh, go along with you both and leave me in peace," growled the colonel. "If we are to leave for Lincoln this afternoon, there's a whole lot of paperwork to be done. Bellswinger!" he barked on the intercom.

"Yessir!"

"Send me Quartermaster Garble. And muster the men for embarkation. Make sure there's none of them left fossicking about on the station platforms. We depart at two sharp!"

"Yessir. What about the men's dinner, sir?"

"Mrs. Churt must serve it in transit."

"Mrs. Churt won't say thank you for that," remarked Bellswinger, when he had replaced the receiver. "You'd best stop polishing buttons, lovey, and go give her a hand."

Nodding, Sauna laid a folded mess-jacket with brilliantly polished buttons on a pile of fifteen others and rose to her feet. As she did so, the phone rang again.

"*Now* what does His Nibs want?" mumbled Sergeant Bellswinger, snatching the instrument off its hook.

But this time it was not the colonel.

"Sauna, Sauna, I want to speak to my little Sauna!" came a high, strident, queerly disembodied wail from the mouthpiece. It seemed as if the phone itself were speaking, rather than a real, live human being far away.

"Bless my buttons, girl, whoever can that be?" grunted the sergeant, greatly astonished. "And how in the world come she's got on to our internal line?"

Sauna had turned white as pipe clay. Her teeth chattered.

"It—it sounds for all the world like my Auntie Floss!" she gulped. "B-b-but how *can* it be? She can't be on the train! Nobody knows what happened to her . . . I thought she was dead!"

"*Sauna! Sauna! Come to your loving auntie!*" wailed the phone.

"Shouldn't you better speak to her, girl? Ask her maybe where she is?" suggested Bellswinger, holding out the receiver. Sauna gave him a desperate look. The very last thing she wanted was to be back in touch with her Auntie Floss—but she could see that Bellswinger thought she ought to take the call, expected her to do so—and therefore, with great reluctance, she took a step forward, holding out her hand for the mouthpiece. But the instant before she reached it, the sergeant shuddered from head to foot with a violent jerking movement and dropped the receiver, which smashed to pieces on the metal floor. Oddly enough, even after the telephone had shattered sound continued to come out of it for several minutes—or perhaps the sound came not from the phone but from the wall and ceiling nearby.

"*Sauna! Sauna! I'm up in the north country. I want you so badly. So ba-a-a-dly! Come to your grandfather's house! At Glen*

Grief! Your great-great-great-great-grandfather's house. Come! Oh, come!"

The voice rose to a frenzied shriek, then faded away.

"Blimey!" gasped Sergeant Bellswinger, picking himself off the floor where he had collapsed after the convulsion shook him. He flopped heavily on to a chair and blew out a long breath. "Blimey!" he said again. "That was an electric shock, that was. Like a bolt o' lightning. Did *you* feel it, gal?"

Sauna shook her head.

"No, but I saw you, Sergeant," she said. "It was awful! I thought you was a goner, for certain sure!"

"Was that voice your Auntie Floss?" he demanded. "Or—or who? If not her, *who?"*

"I dunno, Sergeant! I suppose it could have been Auntie Floss—after all, I ain't got nobody else, but she never called me her little Sauna before. Never! She called me Gal, or You, Whatsyername, and she never in her whole life said she wanted me badly. She never wanted me at all! She only took me a'cos Mam and Dad were dead and there was no one else to take me. She often told me that. She said it was a right pain having to have me in her house. And," said Sauna shivering, "if she wasn't killed by the Snark, where is she? In the north country? Where's that?"

"There's summat pesky rum about it all," grunted the sergeant. "But, anyway, she's off the line now. And that's just as well. You don't have to answer her. You run to Mrs. Churt, gal, and on your way tell Corporal Nark to come along and repair this-ere phone."

Sauna found Dakin with Mrs. Churt, helping to chop up spinach and sassafras which had been snatched from the marshes round Manchester under covering fire.

"It'll have to be soup for the boys' dinner," Mrs. Churt

was saying. "But *thick* soup, mind you, so it won't get all splashed about when the train picks up speed. It's lucky I've got plenty of lentils. Now, Sauna, what are you looking so down in the mouth for, all of a sudden?"

"I had a message from my Auntie Floss, what we thought was took by a Snark."

"And she weren't after all? Where is she, then?"

"Up north, she said. She asked me to go to her—but she never gave an proper address. Except something about Grief. She sounded *ever* so queer."

"Well, we are going up north, by all accounts," said Mrs. Churt—for, of course, news of the troop movements had already flashed about the train like lightning—"so you needn't trouble your young head about that. Maybe she'll get in touch again. Nothing you can do about it till she does."

"But, Mrs. Churt," said Sauna, "I don't want to go back to her. I don't like her. I like it much better on this train."

"She's your auntie, though," pointed out Mrs. Churt. "She took you in. She didn't have to."

"I wish she hadn't! I'd sooner have gone to an orphanage!"

"You can't prove that," argued Dakin. "For you don't know what the orphanage might have been like."

"Anyway, perhaps your auntie wasn't used to children," suggested Mrs. Churt.

"I reckon she wasn't."

"Yet she did put up with you. You gotta remember that."

"Only just," said Sauna. "And I can't think why she wants me back now. I'm not even sure if that really was her voice. It sounded so squeaky and queer."

"Who else could it have been?" asked Mrs. Churt unanswerably. "Still and all, dearie, you don't have to live with her

if you don't want to. Nobody can oblige you, not these days."
Sauna nodded in relief, and they got on with making the
men's dinner. Then all of a sudden the *Cockatrice Belle*, which
had been stationary for so long, gave herself a gentle twitch,
a slow heave like a cat stretching and slipped off along the rails
in a south-easterly direction.

"Oooo!" cried Sauna, enraptured. "We're moving! We're
really moving!"

"Don't get your feathers in a twitch," Dakin teased her.
But he too was filled with excitement and joy at being on the
go again after remaining in one spot for so long; and all along
the train there were loud sounds of the soldiers' joy at the
prospect of change and action. And new recruits who had
come on board at Manchester to replace the men lost in battle were being told by their mates of the pleasures in store.

"We're rolling, we're rolling!"

"Huzza!"

"Ho, ho, jubilo!"

The whole train rang with shouts of enthusiasm as it
came out of the underground station. And, overhead, the
massed clouds of Snarks and Telepods, who had been circling
aimlessly, began to concentrate their movements and to make
vicious repeated dives at the snaky moving object. Sergeant
Bellswinger bustled up and down the corridor briskly re-
minding the men that they were now much more at risk and
must keep a sharp look-out every minute of the time in case
a stray beak or talon or a razor-edged tusk or spine penetrated
the train's outer armour.

Indeed a swarm of Flying Hammerheads carried off Ensign Peascape and Corporal Hunt when they leapt off the
train to change the points at Buxton; this made a grim, if salu-
tary reminder of the dangers that surrounded them. Chester-
field was an empty, ravaged city with not a soul to be seen in

its grass-grown streets or among its battered houses; they hurried through without stopping. The bent church spire had been bent even more and a large Bycorn was to be seen, twined around it. This made the colonel so indignant that he had a trench mortar fired at it, but this merely dislodged a piece of the spire without dislodging the Bycorn.

Dusk had fallen by the time they reached Lincoln, and the *Cockatrice Belle* crept cautiously and quietly into the station, which had been fortified and made into a kind of castle. Some Snarks and Telepods had to be despatched before it was safe for the mayor and corporation to welcome Colonel Clipspeak and his troops, but Lincoln had not suffered so severely as Manchester and the citizens were in better shape. Stores were waiting ready to be loaded on board.

"We get supplies smuggled up canals from the coast," explained the mayor, Sir Lionel Dritch. "Fish and seaweed. Only difficulty is, the smell of the seaweed attracts the Footmonsters. That's what we suffer from worst, here. They fly upside down, you know, with their foot in the air; and their sense of smell is so sharp that one of 'em can locate a single rotten egg on Spurn Head light."

The townspeople of Lincoln were so happy to be visited that they had arranged a gala reception in the station for the crew of the *Cockatrice Belle*, with smoked herring roes served on slices of dried turnip, candied salt beans, and a fearsomely potent drink made from distilled seaweed.

"Upon my word, that is stingo stuff!" said Colonel Clipspeak to Sir Lionel, and he issued an order on the spot that none of his crew were to take more than two glasses of it, and Driver Catchpole only one.

The party was a great success. There were more children

in Lincoln than in many English cities, due to the fact that the Footmonsters, very short-sighted beasts, were unable to see any prey less that one and a half metres in height or forty-two kilos in weight. In London and Manchester it was rare to meet anybody under twelve, but in Lincoln Station there were forty pupils from a mixed junior school waiting to greet Dakin and Sauna, who had a fine time describing life on the train to an admiring audience.

Meanwhile Sir Lionel introduced Colonel Clipspeak to his new passenger, Dr. Wren, the Archbishop of Lincoln.

Archbishop Wren was a cheerful little round man ("More like a robin than a wren," whispered Sauna to Dakin, looking along the station platform).

"Sad times we live in, sir," said Colonel Clipspeak. "Sad times indeed. But we are delighted to have you as a passenger."

"Oh, I don't know, Colonel," said Dr. Wren cheerfully. "I think I'd call them *rousing* times. A challenge to us all. And how splendidly you are responding to it!" He cast a glance of admiration at the glittering train.

"But I understand you have lost a great many of your clergy, Archbishop?"

"That is true, Colonel, but it puts the others on their mettle, you know! I have some excellent young vicars in homemade Snark masks who venture about the countryside putting heart into the people. No, no, I feel this invasion of monsters is sent to test us, and I sincerely believe that we shall pass the test!"

He beamed at the colonel and took a large swig of seaweed toddy.

"Sir," said Major Scanty anxiously, "I think we should be embarking. We ought to leave before midnight and—

ahem—I fancy that some of the men have already exceeded
their two-glass ration."

"You are right, major. Bellswinger! Tell Catchpole to
sound the recall."

Sad farewells were exchanged, and Dakin carried the
archbishop's luggage on board and deposited it in the cabin
that Lieutenant Frisbeen had been obliged to vacate.

"Thank you, thank you, my boy," said Dr. Wren, following him. Dakin observed that the archbishop had a round
domed head, mostly bald, except for a fringe of brown hair,
and bright brown eyes, and walked with a decided limp. This,
as he explained to Dakin, was due to the poisoned sting of a
Basilisk, which had cornered him in the cathedral close.

"How did you escape it, sir?" asked Dakin, dumping a
heavy bag of books (all the archbishop's luggage seemed to
consist of books).

"The very best way to elude the Basilisk, like the Mirkindole—they belong to the same family—is to turn round and
stare hard at it over your shoulder. That generally does for
them at once. It does require some resolution, however. And
very often there isn't time," sighed the archbishop. "The
Mirkindole of course is far more dangerous. Thank you,
thank you, my boy." He offered Dakin a coin, but Dakin said,
"Thank you, sir; we don't really have much use for money
on the train. In fact, not at all. What I'd really like, sir—if it's
not an impertinence—"

"What is that, then? Ask whatever you like?" said Dr.
Wren kindly.

"Might I have a read of some of your books?"

"My dear boy! Of course you may," said the archbishop,
greatly touched. "I know how you feel, for I never travel anywhere without books. Here, have one now." And he fished

out *The Decline and Fall of the Roman Empire.* "There! That should keep you going till our next stop."

"Oh, sir! Thank you!"

Dakin went bounding off down the corridor as if his heels were on springs.

"Look what he's lent me!" he said to Sauna in the galley. "You can have a read of it too!"

"That's funny," said Sauna, looking at the title page. "Now it comes back to me that when I used to get glimpses of you at Auntie Floss's place sometimes you were carrying a book like that under your arm. . . ."

Chapter four

When the Cockatrice Belle left Lincoln, snow was beginning to fall, wafted in over the Lincolnshire wolds by a bitter wind from eastern Siberia. Fierce little flakes stung and clung; they climbed and caked on the windows; and Dakin sighed as he thought of all the extra cleaning and polishing that would be necessary the next day.

"But this weather should help to discourage the Snarks," said Major Scanty, rubbing his hands together as he looked at the snow piling against the windows of the officers' mess.

"Just so long as we don't get derailed or stuck in a drift on our way to Nether Broughton," muttered the colonel pessimistically. "Or so long as the expeditionary force don't get lost in the blizzard."

"Who are you thinking of sending out, sir?" enquired Lieutenant Upfold.

"Well, let me see. Bellswinger had better be in charge of

the main party. At least fifteen men will be needed; they can be in charge of two Gridelin hounds a piece. Bellswinger knows the country, apparently; he says he used to stay with cousins in Willoughby when he was a lad."

Upfold looked disappointed; he had hoped to be given command of the troop.

"You can lead the relief force, Upfold, should one be needed," the colonel told him kindly, and Upfold's face brightened up.

The monsters to be found on these uplands were unfamiliar to the men; they were mostly Sphynxes and Gorgons. Being of southern origin they were not very active or mobile in such wintry weather, and made no serious attacks on the train until it had crossed the River Trent and was climbing into hilly country again.

But at Nether Broughton, where they stopped to refuel with cakes of condensed diesel, there was a sharp, pitched battle with Griffins and Hydras who came coiling up off the track as Lance-Corporal-Engineer Pitkin was performing the hazardous operation of sliding diesel bricks out of the aluminium containers slung under the officers' mess truck. The monsters were finally routed by means of flame-throwers, but not without loss of life and a broken glass panel in the driver's cab.

"We'll need to replace that before we can move, sir," said Ensign Driver Catchpole. "Can't drive 'er along with all the weather a-blowing into the cab."

"How long will it take?"

"Matter of a couple of hours, sir."

"In that case," said the colonel, "we had best send the expeditionary party to Willoughby from here, while the work is put in hand. What do you say, Bellswinger?"

"I'd say yes, sir. It can't be more than eight or nine miles to Willoughby from here. And the climatic conditions are helpful."

If helpful, the climatic conditions were not enjoyable. A zipping blizzard was sending horizontal skeins of snow like wire whiplashes into the men's faces. While the expeditionary party were putting on waterproof boots and fur-lined mitts and Balaclavas under their Snark masks, Bellswinger said to the colonel, "Can I take drummer boy Dakin Prestwich along, sir?"

"In heaven's name, what for? You won't be needing a drummer."

"No, sir, but it struck me—these hounds we're a-going for to fetch have all been reared in Germany, right? And it's all Nottinghamshire to a nutmeg that they won't understand English words of command."

"Humph," said the colonel after a pause. "I hadn't thought of that. But what use will Prestwich be in the circumstances?"

"The lad's a fluent German speaker, sir. On account of how it seems he spent two years underground in the strongroom of Barclays Bank, Shepherd's Bush. While he was there he learned German from two old lady schoolteachers who happened to be taking shelter there too."

"Oh, I see. Very well. You may take him along. Corporal Nark!"

"Yessir!"

"While the party are gone I want you to construct thirty strong, roomy dog kennels for the Gridelin hounds that we shall be taking on board."

"Er, yessir. How bit will the hounds be, sir?"

"Major Scanty says they are about the size of an Irish wolf-hound—that is, about one metre high at the shoulder. And length in proportion, naturally."

"I see," said Corporal Nark. He scratched his head. "And you want thirty kennels. And where are these kennels to be put, sir?"

"Why," said the colonel, "they will have to go in the men's mess."

"I see, sir . . ."

Meanwhile Dakin, interrupted in his eager perusal of chapter five of *The Decline and Fall of the Roman Empire*, was joyfully hauling on gloves and boots and Snark mask.

"Oh, Dakin!" said Sauna, rather upset at his suddenly being whisked off like this on active service. "You will be careful, won't you? Don't forget that the baby Griffins are the nastiest. Their teeth are poisonous."

"Don't you fret your head, I'll be careful," said Dakin, giving her a hasty hug. "And I'll bring you back a Gridelin hound for your very own." He seized his drum and bounded away. ("For you might as well bring the drum along," Bellswinger had said. "The monsters don't like the rat-a-tat one bit, and my guess is that it may be helpful to have covering sound while the hand-over is taking place.")

"You know your route, Bellswinger?" asked the colonel.

"No problem, sir. We just follow the line of the Mink Canal. It runs due east from Nether Broughton to Willoughby."

"Why is it called the Mink Canal?" Dakin enquired, trotting along through the howling snowy dark between Bellswinger and the flat inky water of the Cut which kept swallowing the snow as if it were endlessly thirsty.

"Why, matter o' forty years ago, long before all this hullabaloo with monsters, there used to be a big mink trade between the Norfolk Broads and Ireland—mink was the fashion just then in Dublin and Cork. As there was all those wild mink running loose down in Norfolk, they used to catch

them and ship them by the Cut straight across to Portmadoc.
And on to Ireland. Take *that*, you ugly brute!" he broke off
to aim his Snark gun at a Wyvern which was stalking them.

Croaking, transfixed, it splashed down into the canal.

"So, no question, that's the way they'll have brought
these-here hounds. Train from Germany, submarine to the
Wash, canal boat on from Boston. Now you watch out, my
boy, there's a whole posse of Footmonsters ahead."

The Footmonsters were easy enough to tackle with electric prongs, which overthrew and unbalanced them in their
flight; being such top-heavy creatures, once they had fallen
into the water they almost inevitably drowned.

So battling doggedly against intermittent opposition and
dreadful weather—mixed monsters, wind, snow, and sleet—
the party proceeded to Willoughby-on-the-Wolds, which
had once been a handsome little town with a spacious view
north, east, and west. Now it lay in ruins; shattered walls were
crusted with snow, which also lay thick and untrodden along
the approach roads; and the broken church tower rose up like
an empty candlestick in the middle of the deserted churchyard.

"But it's Willoughby, all right," said Bellswinger, when
they reached the outskirts after a two-hour jog. "I remember
it from when my dad's cousin Samson used to live here.
There was a fine old inn called the Drum and Gaiters; right
by the canal, it used to be. Keep moving, lads; once we stop,
the 'trices start to gather like wasps round a jam jar."

But as they approached the graveyard a troubling sound
greeted them: a sad and eerie howling which seemed to issue
from somewhere in the middle of the village.

"Sounds as if it might be coming from the church," muttered Bellswinger. "Look sharp, lads! The monsters are
mustering thicker and thicker. Dakin, you best beat a rally.

Ensign Noggs 'ull keep you covered. Seems there's plenty of mischief ahead."

Indeed, when they rounded a corner and came within view of the churchyard, a terrible sight met their eyes—for just at that moment a large black snow cloud slipped away from in front of the moon, whose rays displayed everything in stark black and white. The churchyard was all scattered with corpses—Dakin wondered if there were not more bodies lying on the trampled snow than were buried in the graves beneath it. He gazed in fright and horror, still mechanically rattling away on his drum. Men, dogs, and monsters lay strewn all over such other in awful confusion.

"Saints preserve us!" muttered Bellswinger, staring about him. "Look at them all! Looks like every single dog's been done in. And all the folk, too."

"But I thought these dogs were champions at fighting Snarks?" said Dakin.

"So they are. (Don't stop your tattoo, boy; these pesky critters are mustering up above, like gulls to a shipwreck.) But there's Basilisks, too, here; you can always tell; see, those are Basilisk prints in the snow."

He pointed to a huge three-toed print.

"No dog—*nothing*—can stand up to *them*. Keep together, boys! Guard each others' backs. Aim outwards! Make for the church. There's still some Basilisks about—you can tell by the whistling."

Embattled, struggling, keeping close together, fighting for their lives, the group made for a door in the church tower and stood with their backs against it, Dakin all the time whacking away on his drum like a demented woodpecker, while the monsters swooped overhead, and dived, and pounced, and made racing attacks across the snow with outstretched wings and clashing beaks, but then paused and

backed away, annoyed and alarmed by the staccato vibrations.

"*Help!*" called a faint voice from inside the church door, and again they heard that lugubrious howl. Could there be a dog inside there? "*Help . . .*"

"Let us in, then!" shouted Bellswinger, pounding on the door with the handle of his Hydra hammer.

And the door at last swung open and they all tumbled through into darkness, one on top of another, with Dakin desperately wrapping himself round his drum in order to protect it from other people's Snark prongs.

"Who's here?" called Bellswinger.

The answer came in an exhausted feeble murmur from somewhere at floor level.

"Tom Flint, Canine Rescue Mission."

It was followed by a series of weak, melancholy barks.

"What's been going on in this town?" demanded Bellswinger, as the troop gradually sorted themselves out, and somebody had the sense to fetch and light up a battle-flare, which illuminated the scene with a greenish glow.

They found that they were in the vestry, at the west end of the church under the bell tower. It was an empty stony chamber. Everything portable had long ago been removed. A stone stair climbed the wall to a trapdoor hole, which presumably led to the belfry.

"Bells!" said Sergeant Bellswinger, looking up. "Monsters can't stand bells. Are there bells still in this tower, Tom Flint?"

"How would I know?" mumbled the thin, tattered man who had let them in. "I only came to this place for the first time today. And I never want to see it again."

"Well, we better find out," said Bellswinger. "You, Prestwich, you look good for a few pulls on a rope—Brag, Minch,

Coldarm, Forby, Wintless—up those stairs at the double and let's see if we can give the brutes a bit of a ding-dong."

The men, with Dakin, clattered up the stairs to the belfry above, and were relieved to find long, dusty, beaded bell-ropes dangling down through holes in the ceiling. The bells themselves must be in a yet higher loft, out of sight.

"We better hope they're still up there and no metal-eating monster's munched 'em up," said the sergeant, giving a tremendous heave on the rope nearest him. A solemn clang responded from above. "Right, boys! Give those critters out there a real concert. One, two, three—*pull!*"

They pulled with a will. And the bells began to reply in a brassy, chaotic chorus. The men heaved, and dragged, and swung, and swore, and hauled, and jerked, until they were first hot, then dizzy with fatigue. Luckily there were only nine bells, and twenty men had managed to survive the trek along the canal and the skirmish in the churchyard. As one ringer grew too dizzy to go on, another climbed up, tapped him on the shoulder and took over his rope.

The noise they made was tremendous.

When somebody relieved Dakin of his rope he crept carefully down the stone stairway and sat wearily on the bottom step. His knees would only just hold him, and his head rang and sang with the row that was going on up above.

Slowly he looked about him. A few of the men had lit a small fire. Dakin wondered where they had found the wood for it. Could they have used pews from the church? He did not like to ask. They had brought out carrots and parsnips and rolls spread with mushroom paste, which Mrs. Churt had supplied for the expedition, and were toasting these at the flames.

Dakin looked about for the man who had let them in. Tom Flint. There he was being offered a toasted roll by Ensign Quickstep. He took it slowly and stared at it as if he were too tired to bite.

Then Dakin's eyes opened wide for, beyond Tom Flint, in the shadows, he noticed for the first time a great beast, the largest dog he had ever seen in his whole life.

"Is that a Gridelin hound?" he asked Fred Coldarm, who sat on the floor beside him wearily chewing on a toasted carrot.

"Reckon so. Couldn't be owt else, could it? He's a big feller, ain't he? Pity there's only one of 'em left—after we come all this way, and took all this trouble."

"Mind you," put in Private Wintless, who sat beyond him, "if there'd a been thirty of those Gridelin hounds—like there was supposed to be—dear knows where we could find space for them on the old *Belle*. Ask me, it's just as well there's only one left."

"But what went wrong? I thought these dogs were supposed to be hot stuff against monsters?"

"That feller there, Tom Flint, he said it was summat to do with the customs inspector at Boston. A man called Coaltar. Listen: he's telling how it was that chap's fault."

Dakin went over to squat by the fire and listen as he munched his roasted parsnip.

"There was fifteen Hanoverian dog-handlers with the troop," explained the doleful Tom Flint. "And they'd had instructions to come all the way on the canal boat and see the dog-pack handed over to your lot, and give proper directions for feeding and exercise and words of command and all that. But that Coaltar, the harbourmaster at Boston, he wouldn't let the Hanoverians come ashore off their submarine. Very toploftical, he was. Said they'd got the wrong papers, or summat, and he couldn't authorize 'em to go no further . . . One o' those jumped-up nobs in office he is, acts as if his hair is hung with diamonds. So the poor German dog-handlers was real upset, for they said nobody would know how to give the dogs their orders, and the beasts wouldn't understand owt that was told 'em in English. (And nor they could, as it turned out.) But that didn't cut any ice with His Nibs Mr. Coaltar at Boston. All he would do was send for me and my six mates at the Boston Canine Rescue Mission and tell us we were to accompany the dogs in the canal boat. So the Hanoverians— real furious-mad, they were, I've never seen coves so upset— they give us some written notes on a bit o' paper, diet rules and all that, words of command—and then back they had to go, back on their submarine."

"What happened to your six mates from the mission?" asked Bellswinger, who had come down the stairs at this moment, having been relieved by Ensign Priddy.

The bellringing up above was slowing down and becoming more fragmented.

Tom Flint gave a wretched glance towards the door.

"Out there. All of 'em bought it," he said simply. "I saw Ern munched up by a Bandersnatch. And Sam Todd was cut in half by a Hammerhead . . . And the poor dogs was just outnumbered and demolished and *done for*—without anybody to give 'em the proper orders—it was a right shambles, I can tell you. And some chaps from the village turned out to help us, but they was all cut down too—"

He took a gulp of parsnip wine, which somebody had passed him, and coughed miserably.

"So now there's just one of the dogs left?" said Bellswinger. "What's his name?"

"How would I know?" grumbled Tom Flint. "We never got introduced."

Dakin began to feel rather impatient with Tom Flint. Certainly it was a sad and shocking tale he had to tell. Dakin thought how much he would like to see Mr. Coaltar the Boston Harbourmaster compelled to jump off a high tower or swallowed up by a Bandersnatch. But just the same he felt that Tom Flint might have made a bit more effort to look after the hounds left in his care, and get to know them. After all, the trip on the canal boat must have taken at least a day.

"What were the words of command on the bit of paper the handlers gave you?" Dakin asked Flint.

"Bless me, boy, I've forgot what they said, after all that ruckus out there. And that scrap of paper's halfway down some Wyvern's gullet by now."

"Why don't *you* have a go at the poor beast," Bellswinger suggested to Dakin. "See if you can get in touch, perk him up a bit? He looks mighty sorry for himself."

"Not surprising, seeing all his friends have been killed off," said Wintless.

"And he's cut about a bit himself, poor old feller," said Dakin.

He went and knelt in front of the enormous dog, who gazed back at him mournfully. The animal was covered in thick, rough, grey fur, and had a long, curved tail. His ears were upstanding and lined with white whiskers. His eyes, under tufted brows, were hazel-brown, and the tip of his nose was black. His front legs were about the length and thickness of Dakin's arms. He was somewhat clawed and battered, and there was a smear of blood down his chest. But none of the wounds seemed to be too serious. It was grief and shock that had done the worst damage.

"Would you like something to eat, you poor old boy?" Dakin asked him in German.

The dog slowly wagged his tail. His eyes brightened just a little.

"Anybody got a spare mushroom roll? No? Oh well, you may as well have mine. Here—"

The mushroom roll vanished in a snap of enormous jaws and a lengthy pink tongue.

"Stand up, *aufstehen Sie*, and let's have a look at you," Dakin suggested, still in German.

Obediently, the great dog rose to his feet. All the men were now watching in interested silence.

"Looks like Dakin's got on his wavelength all right," somebody murmured.

"That's all very fine—but what's the use of *one* hound?" said Coldarm.

"Better than none!" snapped Bellswinger. "Can you make him sit down again, boy?"

"Sit," Dakin told the dog in German. And he sat.

"Clever old fellow!" Dakin rubbed the dog's bushy eyebrows and bony skull. "You're a real brainy one, aren't you? And I'm sorry as can be about all your friends . . . *Wie heissen Sie?* Hey! There's a bald patch in behind his eyebrow. No it isn't, it's been shaved. And there's something tattooed there; marks. Can you hold the light closer this way, Fred?"

When Fred Coldarm held the light near the dog's head, it could be seen that the marks tattooed on his skin were letters. Dakin traced them over with a careful finger.

"U-L-I. Uli. Is that your name, Uli?" he asked the dog.

Gravely the great creature stood up again, lifted an enormous right paw, and laid it in Dakin's hand.

A spontaneous round of clapping broke out among the men.

"I reckon you got yourself a friend, Dakin," said Coldarm. "Hey, listen—the bellringing's stopped upstairs. D'you think they've all dropped dead of heart failure up there?"

"I wouldn't mind taking another turn," said Dakin, and ran up the stairs, followed by Bellswinger and several others. But when they reached the belfry they saw that the ringers had their faces pressed eagerly against the slit windows.

"Daylight's come at last—or almost!" said Forby joyfully. "And there ain't near as many monsters about. Sergeant, don't you think it's time we made a break for it?"

"You ain't so daft as you look, Forby," the sergeant told him, peering out. "And it's snowing like blazes again, that cuts down visibility. Let's go . . . Hey, see who's followed us up!"

The great dog Uli had climbed the stairs behind Dakin, and now came to stand with his head pressed against Dakin's knee.

"I doubt we're going to have trouble getting him down again, though," said Bellswinger . . .

The trip back from Willoughby-on-the-Wolds to Nether Broughton took less time than the outward journey, since it was undertaken in daylight. But it was no pleasure. The wind was against them, and a slashing snowstorm beat in their faces all the way. Several members of the party, blinded by snow and sleet, fell into the canal and had to be rescued by the dog Uli, who proved a valuable asset.

"Uli! Fetch that man out of the water!" was Dakin's continual shout.

"Worth his weight in ruby rings, that dog's going to be," commented Sergeant Bellswinger.

"Who wants ruby rings? Worth his weight in mushroom rolls, more like," said Dakin, who was hollow with hunger as he had given his rations to the dog.

Tom Flint, from the Canine Rescue Mission, accompanied them, since all his companions were dead and he could not manage the canal boat single-handed. Nothing could be done about the inhabitants of Willoughby-on-the-Wolds, who had come to the aid of the men and dogs and had been killed by monsters. Such as had not been devoured overnight now lay under several feet of snow.

"We can't do owt for 'em, poor devils," said Bellswinger. "Colonel's going to be in a black rage over this job o' work. Let alone we lost ten good men, and only come back with one dog out o' thirty, we wasted valuable time turning south, when we might have been on our way to the Kingdom of Fife. And then—I dunno—the whole thing seems to me like a put-up job. Almost an insult, you might say."

He was talking to Ensign Quickstep, but Dakin, who was jogging beside them through the gale, with Uli close at his heels, heard what he said and asked, "Do you think it was an ambush, Sergeant?"

"Ah, boy, I do. There ain't been such a concentration of monsters seen since we ran in to Manchester—no one's a-going to tell me they come there by accident. That was a planned incident."

"You don't think the people who sent the dogs planned it?" Dakin said in horror.

"No, no, lad, I ain't saying that. But somebody got wind of where we was going, and *somebody* sent the monsters there to lay in wait. And what I'd like to know is, where is that somebody, and how did they hear tell of secret command post orders? That's what I'd like to know. Those Basilisks weren't there by chance. Basilisks ain't so common—not in such numbers as that. There's summat fishy about it."

Somebody has to be a traitor, thought Dakin. But who? What a horrible thought.

He trotted on very soberly through the wintry weather.

*   *   *

A faint exhausted cheer rose up from the expeditionary force when they finally rounded a windswept corner of beech coppice and beheld the *Cockatrice Belle* ahead of them, couched snugly in a deep railway cutting. The tinsel and the red and green glass bells which adorned the train when they first set out from London had long since been smashed or stripped away in battle, but the train was still a gallant sight with its bronze armour-plating and gold stripes, and Lieutenant Upfold had kept the men who remained on board hard at work polishing the windows and cleaning out the wind-vanes in case their returning comrades should be pursued by hostile forces and a speedy departure was required.

An answering cheer came from the garrison on the train as they saw their mates come over the hill, but this died away uncertainly when it became plain that no large pack of Gridelin hounds accompanied the returning force.

Colonel Clipspeak was out on the observation platform with the Archbishop beside him and a guard of sharpshooters with Snark guns.

Bellswinger saluted smartly as soon as he came within earshot, but his tone was sad, flat, and apologetic as he reported. "Have to announce the death of ten men, sir. And the dogs was all killed by monsters before we ever arrived at the rendezvous point. Only this single hound left, what you see, sir."

Clipspeak turned very pale, but remained calm. He said, "You'd best come to my office, Sergeant, and give me the whole story. Let the remaining men of your party be well fed and rested. And the dog had better be taken along to their mess. Who is that civilian?"

"He's a chap from the Canine Rescue Mission at Boston, sir. I'll tell you about him when I make my report. I daresay Mrs. Churt can make him comfortable in the galley till you want to interview him."

"Very well. I don't approve of taking civilians on board, but in the circumstances—and as we have room—" The colonel sighed.

Later, in the office, Bellswinger gave a full account of the disastrous expedition, and the colonel listened with knitted brows.

"You don't think the whole thing was a put-up job? That it was organized from Hanover?" he said.

"No. No, I don't, sir. What for would anyone send thirty Gridelin hounds just to be ate up by monsters? No, what I think was, somebody, somehow, got word of the rendezvous and sent a force of monsters to put a spoke in our wheel."

"Humph," said the colonel, and sat silent for a long time pressing his knobbly fingers together.

"Do you think it can have anything to do with the child Sauna?" he asked at length. "Could she be giving away secrets? And—if so—to *whom?*"

"Well, sir, that's a hard one." Bellswinger frowned. His long red face was very thoughtful. "I don't believe she'd give away our secrets on purpose, sir; that I don't. She's a good girl, and hardworking—Mrs. Churt thinks the world of her, and so does young Dakin and lots of the men—and, besides that, she's as keen as mustard. Keen on our Cause, sir, as you might say. She's learning to handle a Snark gun; she can better some of the men's rounds, six times out of ten, and besides that she's right handy at giving warning of assaults in advance—up to as much as half an hour ahead, sometimes, she can warn us when there's summat nasty coming along. I'd have been glad of her on our trip to Willoughby, and that's a fact. Now I ask you, sir, is it likely that the Other Side would plant somebody as useful as that on us? (If there is an Other Side, as such, which I sometimes take leave to doubt, sir?)"

"You think this invasion of monsters is just a random piece of bad luck, do you, Bellswinger? But what about that memo from headquarters, saying that it's all being *directed* from somewhere up by the Kingdom of Fife?"

"Headquarters ain't always right in their info, sir. Not but what it do seem that some of the things what happen is planned; and planned quite smartly, too," the sergeant acknowledged, sighing.

"Oh, I certainly think they are planned," said the archbishop, who all this time had been sitting in the colonel's easy-chair listening keenly and attentively to the discussion. "I think they are planned," he repeated. "I think that every smallest thing that has befallen us has been planned—even down to the child Sauna's aunt's collection of holiday souvenirs—hundreds of little tiny china pots."

"Sir?" said Bellswinger, greatly startled.

"I have had many talks with the child Sauna, Sergeant, while you were off on your ill-fated errand, and several things have struck me forcibly. One is the nature and character of Mrs. Florence Monsoon. She sounds to me a very strange, not to say repellent and sinister individual. Keeping the child tied up in that manner—keeping her, it seems, *at the behest of somebody else;* no, that situation was not simple, not natural at all. Another significant factor is that Florence Monsoon was not herself a native of Manchester. She moved there when she married. But her place of origin was in Scotland—ah, yes, you can guess where. Not far from the Kingdom of Fife. Near the Pool o' Muckhart. (It is instructive, is it not, that many place names in Scotland relate to streams and water, or to the weather—Burnfoot, Bridge of Earn, Coldrain, Burn of Cambus, Devil's Cauldron—those waters, streams, storms are so important to the Scots.) And Muckhart, of course, lies close to the Ochils, a most mysterious range of hills, volcanic, you know, very abrupt, seamed with unexpected caves and gorges. So your little Sauna, Colonel, is closely connected by her ancestry with the very neighbourhood in Scotland to which you have been directed by your command; is not that a very singular coincidence?"

"Very singular indeed," agreed the colonel gloomily. "In fact it sounds damned fishy to me."

"Not only so," went on the archbishop, "but, according to the child, her aunt had told her stories concerning family forbears which suggest that she can trace her descent straight back to Michael Scott."

"Michael Scott?" said the colonel, perplexed. "You mean the feller that wrote a book called *Tom Cringle's Log*?"

"No, no, Colonel, not that one; a much earlier character, also an author, as it happens, who lived in the twelfth or thirteenth century, travelled to Spain, was an official astronomer (or astrologer; they were synonymous in those days) at the court of the Emperor Frederick II in Palermo and wrote numerous learned books about Nature and her secrets. *Quaestio Curiosa de Natura Solie et Lunae* was one of his bestsellers. And he was reputed to have traffickings with the Evil One, to possess a demon horse and a diabolical ship. When he died, his last and greatest book was said to have been buried with him at Melrose Abbey, lest its secrets fall into unprincipled or inexperienced hands."

"Fancy that, most remarkable," said the colonel, not greatly interested.

"Another of Sauna's ancestors, a more recent one, was a man called John Brugh, a notorious warlock, who lived in Glen Devon around the year sixteen hundred, who was tried and burned for witchcraft."

"Indeed? But I still don't quite see the relevance. What has that got to say to our present predicament?" demanded the colonel fretfully.

"Firstly it explains the girl's psychic powers. These things are often hereditary. They run in families—like red hair and deafness. Secondly, it appears to me that a kind of stage management is going on."

"What *can* you mean, Archbishop?"

"Why—that matters are being put in train to get the girl up to Scotland, up to the neighbourhood of her origin. The aunt mysteriously vanishes, the girl is rescued—quite fortuitously as it seemed at the time, but I now suspect that the whole affair was pre-designed."

"Come to think," the colonel recollected, "there was that funny business of her aunt's voice coming through on the phone. You told me about that, Bellswinger."

"Yes, sir, I did, and a deuced queer start it was. On the internal house line, it was, and smashed the instrument all to little bits, and gave me such a shock as loosened the teeth in my gums. But Sauna didn't like that one little bit, sir, she was even more scared than what I was. She didn't *want* to answer her auntie. And she told me her auntie never loved her, nor wanted her at all, but only took her as there was nobody else as'd have her."

"Yes," said Dr. Wren. "That was what she told me. But in fact, as we now know, the aunt's position was a false one. For Sauna was not alone in the world—she had her cousin Dakin and Dakin's mother in London."

"But what about the dogs?" demanded the colonel. "I must confess, I can't make head or tail of that affair. Who—I ask you—would arrange to have a decent pack of hounds slaughtered *on purpose?*" The colonel had been a foxhunting man in his younger days, so naturally he felt strongly about this. "I can just about swallow your notion that there might have been some deep-laid plot to get the girl aboard this train—though it seems a mighty roundabout way to gain such an end—but why take elaborate steps to do away with all those valuable, high-bred dogs? It don't make sense—no, by Columbus, it don't!"

Dr. Wren sighed.

"There are powers of which our knowledge is minimal," he said. "And *their* values, mercifully, are not the same as ours. We shall just have to be extra watchful, extra vigilant."

"Keep a sharp eye on the gal, you mean?" suggested the colonel.

"Certainly that—among other things. But without making the poor child aware that we do so—for, after all, she herself may be as innocent as the day."

"Well," sighed the colonel, "at all events, we can't put the girl off the train. Besides, she's a deal too useful. Now, what about this other fellow—what's his name, Linch, Finch?"

"Tom Flint, sir, from the Canine Rescue Mission." And Bellswinger told the story of how Flint and his colleagues had been given the charge of the dogs at the port of Boston.

"I wonder," mused Dr. Wren, half to himself, "if the object of the rendevous at Willoughby was to get *Tom Flint* on board?"

"Just wait till I get back and write a report on that bungling harbourmaster," growled the colonel. "All this howdedo results from his idiocy. However! That's water under the bridge. What'll we do with Flint? Can't very well turn him out to walk back to Boston across country on his own?"

"He asks, sir, if he can come with us as far as Queensferry on the Firth of Forth, and then from there he can make his way back along the coast by submarine."

"Seems a bit roundabout—and how did he know we were making for Queensferry?" muttered the colonel. "Still, if that's what he wants . . . Maybe he can be of some use in looking after the hound."

Oddly enough, this reasonable suggestion proved unworkable. Uli, the great, grey, shaggy dog, soon settled down well enough and found his place among the crew of the *Cockatrice Belle;* the men grew very fond of him and competed to slip him bits of their rations (for he had a huge appetite); Mrs. Churt tolerated his presence in her galley, though she did grumble that it was like climbing over the Alps every time she wanted to get to her cooking stove; Dakin and Sauna loved him dearly and spent hours brushing and combing out his shaggy grey pelt and practising the language in which they conversed with him. Sauna called it *Low Hundisch;* very soon she was almost as expert in it as Dakin.

"*Guten* dog, Uli! *Wie geht es?*"

And he would gravely raise his massive right paw.

"*Mitdogessen!*"

And he would stalk hopefully to his dinner-bowl.

But with Tom Flint of the Canine Rescue Mission his behaviour was quite other.

"Perhaps Uli doesn't *want* to be rescued?" suggested Sauna.

Whenever Tom Flint was in his vicinity, the great dog would spring to his feet and growl—a low, threatening, terrible sound. A brilliant green spark would light up in his eyes and he would slowly pace forward, baring two rows of fangs like snowy mountain ranges set in coral-red gums that looked quite capable of crunching an iron bar in half.

To Tom Flint's nervous squeaks of *"All right, then, good doggie!"* he paid no heed at all. A confrontation between the two had never been reached; Tom Flint always bolted.

"I'll tell you what it is," he confided to Sergeant Bell-swinger. "He's come to associate me with that awful battle in the graveyard, when all his mates were killed. It's not to be wondered at he has unhappy feelings connected with me. I daresay it'll pass off, all in good time."

"Unhappy?" said Bellswinger. "Looks like downright un-friendly to me."

"It'll pass, it'll pass. I'll give him a biscuit every now and then, or a bit of Mrs. Churt's raisin cake."

But so far this had not proved successful.

Chapter five

Slowly, in fits and starts, depending on the condition of the track, the *Cockatrice Belle* made her way northwards to York and Thirsk, to Darlington and Newcastle.

Surprisingly few monsters hindered her course. And yet the countryside was sadly empty and wasted; there were very few humans to be seen. Wildlife was considerably reduced too.

"I don't like it," muttered the colonel. "It ain't right, this lack of monsters. I don't trust it."

"You think they are mustering, Colonel, for an all-out assault somewhere farther north?" suggested Major Scanty.

"Yes, Major, that's just what I do think."

And the colonel made Bellswinger keep the men at battle exercises all day long, every day, to maintain them in hard fighting condition. Mrs. Churt was exhorted to feed them on wild spinach, heather porridge, and what raw greens could be garnered by the track-side, either from woods or commons, or from deserted farms and gardens. But as they travelled north the conditions became more and more wintry, snow lay thicker and thicker on hillsides, there were fewer and fewer wild greens to be found.

The main obstacle to their progress in these rougher and more hilly regions was the state of the track, which often required days of repair before the train could cautiously advance over it. Bridges, likewise, needed mending and the engineers had to make use of what materials they could find lying about in ruined goods-yards and sidings along their route.

"Days and days wasted," fumed the colonel, as the party of engineers doggedly extended a new span of bridge across the River Tyne.

"It will be much better on the return journey," mildly pointed out Major Scanty. "Their work will be done already."

"If we ever *do* return," muttered the colonel.

One advantage of these periods of enforced standstill was that Mrs. Churt's herb-gathering parties could range further afield. And the archbishop spent many hours of leisure with Dakin and Sauna, teaching Dakin French, and Sauna the basics of mathematics.

"But why should I want to measure the distance from that tree to the sun?" she asked. "What use would that be?"

"Oh! my dear child! You never know when such knowledge may not come in handy! And," pursued the archbishop thoughtfully, "to have knowledge in your brain of *any* kind, if it is true and factual, is always a useful defence against the assaults of the Evil One. Knowledge is a shield. And it can be a weapon."

"I'm not sure that I know what you are talking about," said Sauna. "In fact, I'm quite sure that I don't."

"Well, my child. Remember those long, sad days in the past when you were imprisoned in your aunt's flat with your hands tied behind you to prevent you from knocking over the china treasures. What did you think about during those hours?"

"Well," admitted Sauna, "at first I used to think of how, if I could get my hands undone, I'd push Auntie Floss out of the window. Or bash her to flinders with the rolling pin. She had one made of marble."

"Just so, Assaults of the Evil One."

"Sir? On Auntie Floss?"

"No, child. On you."

"And then," went on Sauna, pondering, remembering, "I began to see Dakin, ever such a long way off, a-coming to-wards me. And that cheered me up a lot. So instead of planning how to do in Auntie Floss, I took to remembering a place Dad and Mam and I used to stop at on holidays when I was a little 'un."

"Yes? Where was this place then, my dear?"

"I don't know, sir. I don't remember. It was called Bride's Bridge. Two rivers met. And there was a gravel-bed where I used to play. And a ring of trees—big trees. And just a few houses. An old lady called Alison Pittendreich lived there. Aunt Ailie, I called her. She used to give me girdle cakes. And there was big black mountains over the other side of the brook. It was a lovely place. Aunt Ailie gave me two tiny dolls with china heads and I called them Ted and Emily after Mam and Dad. I built them a palace of stones on a big rock in the river. If I think hard, I can remember the sound the water made, running among all those rocks. I used to jump across with dry feet, using them as stepping stones."

"Stepping stones; just so," said the archbishop. "They helped you past the danger of the fast-flowing water. In the same way knowledge, good sound knowledge, can help your mind leap over currents of cruelty, depths of deceit, slimy swamps of sin."

"Fancy!" said Sauna. "You mean knowing about the square on the hypotenuse can do all that?"

They were sitting in the colonel's office; the colonel himself was outside on the observation deck inspecting a party of men who were holding a Snark practice. In the distance they could hear the powerful voice of Sergeant Bellswinger:

"Form THREES!

Snark weapons—TUNE!

Snark weapons—POINT!

Snark weapons—FIRE!

As you were. Reload, Make ready. Breathe—IN!"

Every seven seconds there was a loud crackle as the Snark guns were fired. The archbishop sighed.

"Warfare always seems so simple," he said. "That is why almost everybody falls back on it in the end. It is the dealings and manoeuvrings beforehand that are so dangerous and delicate. And important. Of course we must always hope to avoid open war if we can."

"Even if we are right, and the other lot are wrong?" asked Dakin.

The archbishop sighed again. "But who knows for sure—" he was beginning, when the phone rang.

"Oh dear me, that may be headquarters for Colonel Clipspeak. He was hoping for a call. Would you take it, Sauna, and I will call the colonel—"

But even before Sauna could pick up the receiver, they heard the same nasal whining voice that on the former occasion had echoed round Bellswinger's little office. It seemed to pour at them like smoke out of the wall panels and the furniture and the relief map on the end wall.

"*Sauna! My little Sauna!*"

The dog Uli leapt up, howled miserably and, with ears flattened and tail trailing, bolted precipitately from the room.

"Oh, mercy!" gasped Sauna, much too scared to pick up the phone. The archbishop stretched out his hand for the receiver. "Don't touch it, sir, *don't!*" cried Sauna. "The sergeant did, when this happened before, and he got a real awful shock."

"Sauna! Come to me, come! Come to your grandfather's house! I need you so ba-a-a-adly! I am all alone, and old, and helpless, and crippled. Nobody helps me. I need you to care for me, Sauna! *I* looked after *you*, all that time, I rescued you, I fed you and loved you and was a mother to you—now it's your turn to make a repayment for all I did. For my friends don't come any more—nobody comes—and it's lo-o-o-onely here, it's co-o-o-old. Come to your grandfather's house. I need your young hands to help me. And, if you come, perhaps my friends will come back—ahh-ahh-ahh!"

The words ended in a gibbering shriek.

The archbishop had leapt to his feet and stood listening, all aquiver, like a gundog pointing at a rustle in the leaves. The small plump man suddenly seemed charged with power and a kind of righteous fury.

"Begone! you foul spirit!" he called out in a loud, clear voice. "You have no right in this world. You have no right to make any such demand on the girl. None! Get you gone to your own place!"

". . . Only wanted a little comfort!" whimpered the voice. "So cold—so lonely—all in the dark—no stairs to climb, no light, no smells, no sounds, no tastes, no voices—"

"You have no right to such comforts!" thundered the

archbishop. "You bartered away those rights when you made your bad bargain. You made your own wicked bed and now you must lie in it. Begone! And stop tormenting the child."

Dakin and Sauna stared at one another, open-mouthed and wide-eyed.

The voice died away in faint wails and sobs.

Dr. Wren wiped beads of perspiration from his brow.

"That was very instructive," he said. "Very instructive indeed. I must devote a lot of thought and prayer to this occurrence, my child. Meanwhile—if anything like that should happen again—pay no heed to it! None! Do not even reply. If necessary, clap your hands over your ears to shut out the sound."

"Then—" whispered Sauna, "*wasn't* it my Auntie Floss on the line?"

"It is more likely," said Dr. Wren, "that somebody—something—was impersonating her. Or—if it was your aunt—she has been taken over—possessed—by some external power. So you must on no account take any notice, or even *think* of complying with any of her demands."

"No, sir. Th-thank you."

Uli crawled back into the office, dragging his tail along the floor, whining, very much ashamed of himself. He laid his huge shaggy head on Sauna's knee and looked up at her as if to say, "I do apologize, but really it was quite out of my power to stay in the room with *that* going on."

"SQUAD—disMISS!" bawled Sergeant Bellswinger outside.

"Do you think that *was* Aunt Floss's voice?" said Sauna to Dakin when they were alone together. "You met her, you heard her talk?"

Dakin was doubtful. "I wasn't there for long," he said cautiously. "It sounded sort of like her—but—I dunno. It could have been somebody imitating her voice. That's what Dr. Wren seems to think. And he's a canny old cove."

"But *why* should somebody do that? *Who?*" shivered Sauna. "If it isn't Auntie Floss, who in the world would ask for me to come like that?"

"Well," said Dakin, "best do what Dr. Wren says—take no notice; don't think about it."

"That's easy for you to say! It wasn't speaking to you!"

Dakin reflected that this was true. But he did not know how to help Sauna, and this made him rather impatient.

"*Try* not to think about it. Shall we play a game of checkers?"

"No," said Sauna, "I'd rather read a bit more of that book about Rome."

Reading about what happened in Rome so long ago, she thought, might take her mind off what was happening now.

That night Sauna had a bad dream. She woke up in the cabin that she shared with Mrs. Churt shrieking her head off. She found herself on the floor, having rolled clean out of her bunk, which was the upper one.

At the time the train was stationary, waiting for daylight so as to resume its journey on the relaid track to Newcastle.

Sauna had been looking forward with painful excitement to revisiting the town where she had lived happily with her father and mother until they set off for that ill-fated Spanish holiday. Since then she had never been back. If there was time, Colonel Clipspeak had promised, and not too many monsters about, Lieutenant Upfold might escort her to Dry Dock Street, to look at her former home.

Perhaps it was memories of her previous life that had crept into her head and made her dream.

At any rate she let out such a fearful shriek that it woke every soul on the train. Guards cocked their Snark guns, sentries switched on their battle flares, sleeping soldiers tumbled out of their berths and reached around for weapons, the Colonel shot bolt upright in his bed and shouted for Sergeant Bellswinger on the internal line, alarm bells went off and the dog Uli let out a series of shattering barks.

"What is it, my duck, whatever's the matter?" cried Mrs. Churt, who slept in the lower bunk and had heard Sauna fall past her and land with a thud on the ground shrieking all the while.

"Oh!" gasped Sauna. "It was just a dream—but it was so *awful.*"

Mrs. Churt stuck out a skinny arm and wrapped it comfortingly round Sauna's shoulders.

"Now, now, dearie, don't take on! A dream's only a dream! Here, put a blanket round you and let's us go along to the galley and make ourselves a cup of sassafras tea."

With her teeth chattering, Sauna meekly obeyed. Half the train was awake and stirring by now, and Mrs. Churt had to make about thirty cups of sassafras tea, and find a bowl of marrow broth for Uli, who also slept in her cabin. Sauna had landed on him when she fell, which helped break her fall but left Uli feeling rather hard done by.

"What was the dream about, my child?" asked Dr. Wren, when the startled soldiers had drunk their tea and gone grumbling back to their beds or their watch posts.

"Oh, sir, it was so awful! I was with Mam and Dad and we was going on holiday. In the train. And we came to a station called Douleur. And my Dad said, 'That means sorrow in French'."

"So it does," said the archbishop thoughtfully. "Dolour."

"Well, we all got out at this station with our bags and we got a horse and trap to take us on to where we were going. The place called Bride's Bridge, where we always used to stay. I saw a street sign that said Sorrow Street. And when we got to the place, Mam said to me, You'll want to go and see your Aunt Ailie, while we do the unpacking. She'll give you some of her treacle candy, for sure, or some of her fochabers. (Those were cakes and sweeties that Aunt Ailie used to make.)"

"Yes, my child?"

"So I went along the road to Aunt Ailie's cottage. I could hear the river, rumbling like the sound of gunfire. It was in spate, rushing down between the rocks. And then I came to Aunt Ailie's cottage up the hill—it was a small stone house thatched with reeds and heather—and—and—" Her voice shook. "Oh, it was awful," she muttered.

"*What* was, my child?" The archbishop's voice was comforting but firm.

"Outside the door there was standing—a-a-a thing."

"What kind of a thing?"

"Well, it was shaped like a person—but it was all made of withies, willow wands. Wicker. Like a fence. Bent and twisted into a shape. It was dark brown, you could see right through it, between the wands. Like a—like a lobster pot. There was a shape for the head, and a shape for the chest, and two arms that were just made of several thin wands bunched together and curved into claws for the hands. The ones for the head was all coiled round in a bundle. The hands were springy and dark, almost black—"

"Calmly, take it calmly now, my dear—"

"And down below there was legs coming out from under its skirt. They were all wet and muddy—as if it had waded out of the brook—"

"Gently now, take a deep breath—"

"And it began to walk towards me, it began to raise its arms—and I couldn't stand it, I woke up, yelling—"

"And I don't blame you at all," said the archbishop. "A most disagreeable dream. Terrifying. I should have yelled myself."

"Sir, what does it mean? What *was* that thing?"

"Child, it was nothing but a scarecrow put together to frighten you."

"But it was alive!"

"No, it was a puppet. Or a marionette, hanging on strings—moved by somebody up above."

If Dr. Wren had intended to soothe Sauna by this suggestion he had not succeeded. She whispered, "But then—who was that somebody? Where were they? In the house?"

"Child, child, all this was only your dream!"

"What do you make of that, Mrs. Churt?" said Dr. Wren quietly, when after much soothing and administration of calming potions Sauna had at last been persuaded back to bed.

Dr. Wren and Mrs. Churt had struck up a friendship which began when they found that they shared the same birthday, March the first, and went on when she discovered that he suffered from chilblains, and cured them in half a day with her comfrey ointment. They had discussions on many topics, and the archbishop often did a row in her cross-stitch, while they canvassed such problems as how to deal with hysterics, nightmares, stammering, hiccups, and fear of death.

"Well, sir, if you ask me, they're just trying to scare the girl," said Mrs. Churt quietly. "But she don't scare easy, Sauna don't, if she's given time to pull herself together."

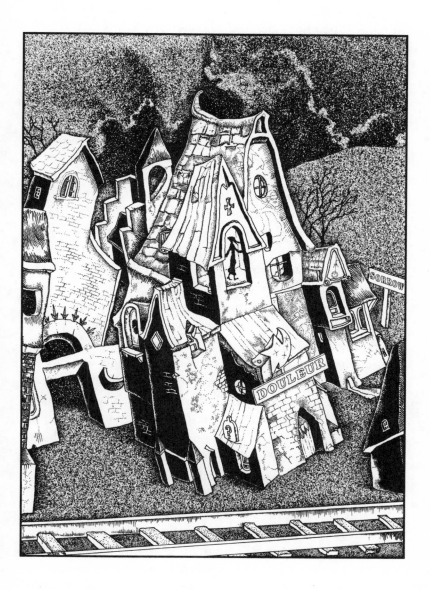

"Ah," said Dr. Wren. Thoughtfully he took a couple of stitches. Then he said, "And who are *they*, Mrs. Churt?"

"Why, sir, the Bad Ones."

Next day the *Cockatrice Belle* crept across the River Tyne and was received with great acclaim and rejoicing by the citizens of Newcastle. The climate so far north was on the chilly side for Snarks, and so there were not a great many of these pests, but the city was much bedevilled by Kelpies and Trolls. Both these monsters were very unpleasant and dangerous. The Kelpies were large, slow-moving creatures with webbed feet, the bodies of horses or cows and human faces; they dripped water and seaweed, devoured any living creature they encountered and were virtually indestructible, as their thick hides turned off all bullets and darts. Trolls were of equally large dimensions. They had hypnotic fiery blue eyes and dynamic powers of self-transportation. They too were omniverous, and had much reduced the population of Newcastle. Their only vulnerable point was that if caught away from home at the moment of dawn they would turn to stone. It was thought they emerged at night from lurking-places in Harwood Forest, some miles north of the city. Sometimes they were entrapped by their own greed if they lingered too long in the streets munching their victims and were overtaken by sunrise. There were quite a number of stone Trolls to be seen in the city of Newcastle, and very hideous they were.

"But there's one advantage," said the mayor, Walter Herdman. "Granted they're not handsome, but they do serve as a useful warning to folk not to loiter about the streets after sunset. And they save the expense of putting up municipal statues—all free, gratis and for nothing." He considered, and added, "Free except for the loss of life, that's to say. But any folk that's ganning about in the streets after dark is most likely to be foolish young harum-scarums and have got only their selves to blame."

He said this to Colonel Clipspeak at the civic welcoming party, which was given for the crew of the *Cockatrice Belle* as soon as she had managed to creep across the reconstructed bridge over the River Tyne.

Newcastle, like Lincoln, had not suffered so severely as Manchester, for the inhabitants had managed to maintain risky contacts with the continent by submarine and so they were not short of food, but the citizens were hungry for news of the south country, and very grateful too for the restoration of their bridge.

Lieutenant Upfold, who was a chemist, had devised a gas made of mustard, ipecacuanha and daffodil juice, which had proved lethal to hordes of Kelpies when they climbed out of the Tyne and hindered the bridge-building crews. The Kelpies had been routed and their numbers greatly reduced while the work was in progress; but, unfortunately, just before the job was finished ingredients for the gas had run out, so it was almost certain that the Kelpies would soon begin to multiply again.

"Daffodil juice is the difficulty," said Upfold. "Now there isn't any chance of restocking until next spring."

"Just think," sighed the mayor, "of the days when we used to be able to import kiwi fruit and daffodil juice from New Zealand. We're really cut off here; we might as well be at the North Pole. But at least now we'll be able to get across the bridge to Gateshead. We are really obliged to you and your men, Colonel."

Sauna was allowed to go off on her nostalgic excursion with Lieutenant Upfold, but it proved a sad disappointment. Firstly, the handsome, busy streets of Newcastle where she had skipped happily along on shopping errands with her mother, or played hopscotch and relievo with friends, were now silent, empty and half overgrown with nettles and grass, lined with dead leaves and crumpled paper. Very few people were to be seen. But there were many ugly, menacing stone facsimiles of Trolls who had been overtaken by daylight at the end of their nightly marauding.

Then, when they reached Dry Dock Street, where Sauna had been born and lived all her life until the plane crash, she found the little row of houses half demolished.

"Looks like Basilisks have been on the rampage here," said Upfold gloomily, staring about at the burnt woodwork and blackened bricks, broken windows, crumbling walls and scorched garden patches.

"Oh! Our house!" wailed Sauna. "Half of it's not there."

It was the one at the end of the row. The roof had fallen in and the interior, which could be seen through broken windows, was heaped high with rubble and masonry; the door hung jammed on its hinges; Sauna had hoped to get inside, but this was not possible.

"I'm glad Mam and Dad can't see it," she said, gulping and wiping her eyes. "Mam used to keep it so nice! And Dad used to paint the door and windows each spring . . . and he grew leeks and sweetpeas in the garden. Oh, why did all this have to happen?" she asked Lieutenant Upfold.

"I don't know, ducky," he answered her sadly. "Dr. Wren says it's human wickedness coming to a head—like a boil that wants lancing—and that things have got to get worse before they can get better."

"I don't see how they *can* get worse." Sauna's tone was despairing. She took a few steps into the tiny front garden, peering rather hopelessly at the muddle of broken bricks and smashed timbers, old bits of rusty iron, draggled cloth and fragments of china that were piled there, higgledy-piggledy.

"I wish I could tidy it up a bit. I hate to see it like this."

"No time for that, dearie. We'd best be getting back to the *Belle.*"

"Oh! What was that?"

A snapping sound, followed by a rumble of falling stones, had come from inside the house.

"Lieutenant! Some person's *in* there!"

"Most likely a rat. Or it could be Echidna or Hydra—come on, lovey, let's get out of here. The colonel would have my teeth for tiddly-winks if I let you run into danger—so would Dr. Wren."

But as he caught her hand, almost pulling her away, Sauna cried out, "Wait! Just a moment!" Under a piece of dirty rag her eye had caught a gleam of red and blue—she pounced and dragged out a small bundle which she hastily tucked into her pocket as Upfold whisked her off along the deserted street.

"We dassn't take chances in these parts," he apologized, glancing quickly around the ruined neighbourhood as they hurried along. "But what was that you picked up?"

"Two things I was very fond of—I'll show you back at the station."

When they were under cover, Sauna displayed her re-claimed treasure. It was a pair of tiny old-fashioned dolls, with China heads and cloth bodies, each of them not much longer than a hand-span. The female had a striped skirt and red crossover shawl, the male a black hat, white shirt, and black trousers, with a blue cravat.

"To think I've come across them!" Sauna said, cradling them fondly. "I was telling Dr. Wren about them only yes-terday."

"Well, I'm glad our trip wasn't quite wasted," Upfold said kindly. "They'll be something to remind you of home—"

"But I wonder who stuck this nasty great pin right through them? I never did *that!*"

The pair of small dolls were skewered together by a kilt-pin, a kind of outsize safety-pin, which was red with rust, and pierced clean through their stomachs.

"It's stuck," said Sauna, tugging at it as they crossed the station.

"I expect it's because the dolls are so damp. They are probably filled with sawdust. You'd better wait till you've dried them off, and then grease the pin a bit," Upfold suggested.

On the platform where the *Cockatrice Belle* had halted they were overtaken by Tom Flint, also returning, it seemed, from a trip round Newcastle. He was out of breath and gulping, as if he had run from some pursuer.

"Are you all right?" Upfold asked him.

"Who—me? Oh—yes—yes; there's naught amiss with me. But this place is a bit of a dismal dump though, ain't it? I see *you* found something pretty, though, love, didn't you?" he added alertly, catching sight of the two little dolls in Sauna's hand. He was about to say something more when a volley of snarls from Uli, who was being exercised up and down the platform by Dakin, caused him to change his mind and hurry off to his own end of the train.

"I can't fathom that fellow?" said Upfold, looking after Tom Flint. "Why doesn't he take a ship home from Newcastle? Instead of coming all the way to Scotland with us?"

"Maybe he has an aunt in Scotland he wants to visit," panted Dakin. "Hey, Sauna! If you've done gadding about Newcastle, d'you want to run Uli for a bit? He's just about worn me out."

"In just a minute. I want to put these in the galley to dry off."

"Well, don't hurry yourself, Your Royal Highness!" Dakin called after her. He felt aggrieved because he had not been included on the excursion to Dry Dock Road.

And when Sauna came back, which she did very speedily, and was greeted by Uli with loving enthusiasm as if she had been away for weeks, Dakin walked huffily away instead of staying to jog up and down the platform with her as he would normally have done.

"What's up, Dakin?" Sauna called, but he did not answer.

He went off sulking to practise his drum, with a blanket spread over the skin to muffle the sound. Sauna looked after him frowning faintly, but then forgot his crossness in her wonder at the discovery of the two small dolls. But who in the world could have stuck that great rusty pin through them? And why? And when?

She must be sure to show them to Dr. Wren. She thought they would interest him very much.

The *Cockatrice Belle* set out on her way again at twilight in order to miss the Kelpies and Trolls. Extremely wild country lay ahead, the Borders and the Cheviot Hills; the people of Newcastle had warned the crew that they would find the track in very bad condition. A lot of repair work would need to be done before they reached Edinburgh and crossed the Forth to the Kingdom of Fife. The Forth Bridge was totally devastated—so it was said—and they would need to turn inland and make a crossing further west.

They began by following the course of the Tyne valley, and then the Upper Tyne, proceeding rather slowly and shining watch-lights ahead up the track. The weather was windless, and very cold; snow lay on the high hills to either side of the railway, and the tracks themselves were furred with frost, although at present there was no snow in the valley.

"But when she do come, she'll be a one-er," said Ensign-Driver Catchpole, shivering in his sheepskin boilersuit. "Ground's so hard, snow'll lie on her like a blanket, and there's bound to be drifting. I wish we could make better speed—that I do."

Unfortunately, arriving at the wayside halt called Falstone, they discovered a big gap in the line.

"The track's been took clear away, sir," Catchpole told the colonel. "For a matter of a quarter-mile ahead. Who could 'a done it, dear only knows. Nor what they'd *want* it for, in drodsome parts like these. It beats me altogether. Lucky we brought a bit o' spare track with us—but it'll take a while to lay."

"Well, there's nothing for it but to start on the work at once," sighed the colonel. "It is fortunate that this area seems to be fairly free from monsters. Set up the arc-lights and tell the plate-layers to get going."

The arc-lights on poles were fuelled by stellar power, and cast a brilliant radiance along the stretch of permanent way from which the tracks were missing. On either side rose steep heather-covered banks, and behind them were the black hills.

"Funny thing," said Bellswinger, staring along the empty stretch of road-bed. "I've seen tracks mangled and I've seen 'em chawed and bent and rusted and burned, but I've never seen 'em took away altogether. Maybe a Bandersnatch come by—I've heard they'll swallow anything. Work as fast as you can, lads."

The men at work on the track needed no urging. The extreme cold was enough on its own to keep them dashing about. Mrs. Churt made gallons of blackberry tea; Dakin and Sauna ran in and out with trayloads of steaming mugs.

"Uli doesn't like it here," said Sauna. "He's nervous. Hear him growl."

"It was because Tom Flint walked by," Dakin said snubbingly. "And because he doesn't like the cold."

Sauna shrugged, and hurried off with hot drinks.

It had been many years since there were station staff at Falstone Halt. The booking-hall stood deserted and dusty. Alongside the station building was a roomy, open-fronted storehouse or cart-shed. Its entrance faced away from the track on to the grass-grown station yard. None of the men at work on the track had been round to that side of the building, or had noticed that in its cover a light carriage and two horses were silently waiting.

At a moment when all attention was focused on the repair work, two hooded men came darting out of the shed, snatched Sauna as she returned to the train with a trayload of empty mugs, dropped a heavy cloth over her head, hauled her into the carriage and whipped the horses into a gallop. Two minutes later they were out of sight, going up the northbound track towards the Cheviot Hills.

The dog Uli set up a fusillade of barking. But he was tied to a rail on the observation platform.

Dakin had witnessed the whole affair and started forwards to do something, help Sauna, prevent what was happening. But a flock of huge, hairy black birds descended on him, pecking, croaking, flapping their heavy wings in his face, clawing at his eyes and impeding his vision; when, scratched and bleeding, he had beaten them off with crossbow and Kelpie knife, it was too late; the station yard was empty.

"Hey! Was that a carriage?" said Corporal Nark, arriving the moment after. He was followed by Catchpole who said, "I thought I heard horses' hoofs?"

Dakin got his breath back and wiped the blood from his eyes.

"Sergeant!" he yelled. "Sergeant! Someone's snatched Sauna! Grabbed her. In a carriage! Two fellows in masks—they ran off with her!"

At first he was not believed.

"Go on, lad, you're imagining things. You're in a proper miz-maze. It was having those ravens come down on you. Take it easy, now. A carriage? *Horses?* In this godforsaken spot? Is it likely I ask you?"

But there were the hoof tracks, Sauna was not to be found anywhere and Uli was howling his head off.

"Colonel's going to be in a rare taking over this," said Bellswinger at last, when all search proved vain; and he was right.

"They have got to be followed. The child *must* be found and brought back," said the colonel.

"But, sir, how? It'd be no manner of use trying to follow them on foot. Not a horse-drawn carriage—they could do fifteen miles an hour. We'll have to wait till the rail track's repaired, and then make inquiries as we go—at Hawick and Melrose and Galashiels."

Gloomily the colonel at last agreed that they had no alternative.

"I wouldn't have had this happen for ten thousand pounds," he said.

At breakfast next morning, when the next section of the track had been completed and the *Belle* crept carefully on her way, it was discovered that Tom Flint, too, was missing from the train.

"*I* could have told *any*body not to trust *him*," said Mrs. Churt, impatiently folding up her cross-stitch.

Chapter six

When Sauna woke she knew that a lot of time must have passed. Days, perhaps. Days and days, even. In some indefinable way, she felt older. Her head ached, her mouth tasted dry and queer and there was a sweet, strong, unpleasant smell in her nostrils, like the smell of the white powder that Auntie Floss used to sprinkle to keep away moths and mice. Somebody had been dreaming, a long, sad, complicated dream, and somebody had been crying bitterly over what had been said in the dream. . . .

After much pondering she realized that the person who had been crying was herself. But I can't remember *who* said *what*, she thought, only that it was someone I knew very, very well. And that it was heartbreakingly sad.

Breathing was difficult, and seeing anything was out of the question, because her head was wrapped in thick cloth. And her hands were tied tightly together. And she felt sick, partly because of the heavy, stuffy cloth and its disgusting smell, partly because of the motion. Jog, jog, jiggle, joggle, joggle.

I can't be on the train, she thought. The train runs smoothly. You just feel it vibrate. Can I possibly be on a ship?

What happened?

Over and over, painfully, she sent her memory back. It was like sending a lazy child to school. She remembered the train slowing down. Because of the missing track. And Mrs. Churt making pints of blackberry tea. Then what? Memory, like the train, slowed down and came to a stop.

Her hands fought against the cords that tied them. She arched her wrists and pulled, and bent her little fingers backwards to push and scrabble, poke and rub at the rope, trying to stretch and loosen it. She would have pushed with her thumbs, which were stronger, but they were too short to be any use and, besides, they bent inwards not outwards. But slowly, slowly, she did begin to feel the cords give a little. Sauna's fingers and wrists were very strong from all the chopping and shredding she had done in the galley with Mrs. Churt, all the grinding and churning, the grating and kneading, and pounding of dough.

She worked away at the cords. It was all she could do.

But still it was a slow and discouraging business. When she grew tired, she tried to push the cloth away from her face with her tied hands. That, too, was a painfully unrewarding job. But she was at last successful in drawing in a sniff or two of air that did not reek quite so powerfully of moth- and mouse-powder. And a blink of grey light showed below the darkness.

The snatched breath of sharp cold air made her more

conscious of the rest of her body and its problems. First, her feet were freezing; they were completely numb and for a long time she wondered seriously if they had been cut or burned off. But her thighs and knees were there, she could feel them. She was sitting uncomfortably on a broad, flat, hard seat, with her legs stuck out straight in front, leaning against a hard seat-back, probably made of wood. Her elbows were pressed against hard objects on each side. A cold draught was blowing on to her chest and shoulders.

Slowly she became aware that she was listening to two voices conducting a kind of dialogue. She was unable to grasp what they said, for they spoke in some unknown language. One spoke much more than the other—an urgent, obstreperous, pleading gabble, on and on and on, like a kitten mewing or a baby crying to be fed.

From time to time, not very often, the second voice would reply with one cold drawling statement on a high note, like the clang of a ship's bell, or the cry of a seabird.

Then the other would start pleading again, gabble-gabble-gabble-gabble. Babble babble.

Can't that one see it's no use, thought Sauna. She was reminded of how, long ago, she used to go to church service on Sundays with Mam and Dad, and some Sundays, not very often, thank goodness, there would be something they called the Litany. She had never liked it; it made her feel unhappy inside, because it seemed to go on and on, asking and asking, and there never seemed to be any answer to all those pleading requests.

You shouldn't *need* to ask for something like that, thought Sauna.

It was the same with the two voices that drifted back to her, alternately louder and softer, on the fitful wind.

If they go on clattering at each other for long enough, perhaps I shall begin to understand what they say.

Listening to them made some distraction from her sufferings. But not much. She was very miserable indeed, in many different ways. She was cold, her head ached, she needed to relieve herself, she was hungry and queasy, she was puzzled, worried about how she was ever to find her way back to the *Cockatrice Belle;* and she was also much troubled in her mind about Dakin. He had seemed almost bad-tempered, almost hostile, the last few times she had spoken to him, and that was not like Dakin at all. What could be the matter with him?

Several things now happened all at the same time.

The two voices rose up to a climax; for a moment it seemed to Sauna that she understood the meaning of what they were saying to each other, although the words remained unfamiliar. But the message was unmistakable.

"Take me with you! Master, take me with you!"

No.

"I beg you, I *beseech* you. I have served you faithfully. I have obeyed your orders. Take me with you."

No.

"Do not, do not leave me here alone. I can't endure it. Take me with you, I beg you!"

No.

Pushing, straining while the voices were so occupied with one another, Sauna finally managed to shove the cloth wrapping off her face and down around her neck.

If she had not been so utterly frozen, hungry and exhausted, she might have let out some kind of gasp. And the course of events might then have gone very differently. But she remained totally silent, in a paralysis of cold and shock.

The first thing she noticed was the light. It was dusk, the strange, pinkish luminous afterglow that sometimes follows sunset. She was in a horse-drawn carriage, travelling fast along a road that ran in the bottom of a valley, between high hills. The hills, thickly wooded, were dark indigo blue, almost black against the lustrous pearly glow of the sky. The sound of a river could be heard very loud, close at hand, rushing among rocks.

In front of Sauna were two figures, the driver of the carriage and another seated beside him; they could only be distinguished as shapeless lumps of darkness in the fast-fading light. *Were* there two, indeed? Sauna could not be certain. Sometimes there seemed to be just one. But there were certainly two voices.

Now the cold voice gave a direction, an order. This must have meant go *left*, for the horses slowed and turned left, proceeding more slowly and gingerly up a rougher, narrower track. Here they were in almost complete dark, under heavy over-arching trees. And the hillsides drew together into a gorge.

Sauna, having freed her head, began to wrestle with greater confidence to loosen the cords round her wrists. Just a few minutes more and perhaps I'll have them free, she thought hopefully; and then what? Would it be possible to open the carriage door and throw herself out? Would she break her legs? Would the driver and his companion hear her? The sound of water was still very loud—there must be a waterfall, crashing down from a height, somewhere close by. The carriage was not moving very quickly . . .

But then it drew to a stop, slewing off the track into a flat area, perhaps a quarry, at the side of the road.

The two voices spoke again: a single brief order from the

cold, distant one, more wild and anguished expostulation
from the other.

"Lord! Don't leave me! Take me with you!"

No.

"I beg you, I beg you, Master!"

Obey me.

Instead of trying to escape, Sauna could not help listening intently. Who *were* they? What could they possibly mean?

So she missed her chance. The door opened, she was
dragged from her place and thrown roughly on to hard, rocky
ground. She hit her head, and lost consciousness for the second time. But before she did so she heard a last agonized,
wailing prayer:

"Do not desert me, Masterrrr . . ."

Then silence.

When Sauna woke for the second time, it was to a truly ferocious degree of cold. She had thought she was cold in the
carriage; but that was balmy warmth compared with what she
now felt. A wild gale was blowing, and the icy bite of
snowflakes on her face might have been what woke her; she
struggled in a sitting position and found with relief that at
least she had the use of her feet and could by degrees clam-
ber up, stand, walk and warm herself. It was night, but not
completely dark; there must be a full moon somewhere behind the snow clouds. She was at the side of a track, a flat bare
place enclosed by woods; behind her rose a sloping cliff, and
on the other side of the track there seemed to be a deep drop
into a gully. Behind the wail of the wind she could hear water
falling. To her right, she saw that the track was blocked: a
huge tree had fallen across it in a tangled confusion of

smashed branches. Perhaps the sound of the tree's fall was what had woken her? It must have happened very recently— some of the branches were still groaning and settling. If I had been twenty yards further that way, I should have been killed, I should have been crushed to death before I woke, thought Sauna, and a strange chill came into her, a chill of mind, not of body, at the thought of the danger that had been so close.

She dragged again at the cords round her wrists, and at last they were loosened enough so that she could twist out first one hand, then the other. She was on the point of throwing away the tangled mess of rope; but then thought better, and stuffed it into her pocket. No telling what might come in handy among these groaning, threshing trees; and in the same thrifty spirit she picked up the length of coarse cloth which had been wrapped around her head. It might once have been the skirts of a man's coat. It still carried that strange, un-pleasant, sweetish smell, but was at least some protection against the weather; she drew it over her shoulders.

Which way had the carriage brought her? It had turned left, she remembered, from the wider road, and then left again into the quarry; logically, therefore, to go back the way she had come she ought to go to her right. But that was im-possible, for the way was completely blocked by the fallen tree. Doggedly she turned in the other direction and followed the track uphill.

I wonder why there are no monsters? Perhaps they don't come out when it snows so hard.

She was too hungry and weak to walk at all fast. But the act of walking warmed her, and she tried once again to re-member what had happened when the *Cockatrice Belle* came to a stop.

The men went ahead to lay a new track. We had stopped in a tiny deserted station. Mrs. Churt made blackberry tea for the fellows working up the track. Dakin and I carried trays of mugs . . .

Somebody must have nobbled me, she realized. When I was taking the tray of empty mugs back to the train. That's as far as I can go; I can't remember any more after that. But why did they do it? What's the point? And, if there *is* a point, why leave me here in the middle of no man's land? What's the point of *that?*

The sound of those two voices hung in her mind's ear: the pleading, beseeching gabble, the cold, distant refusal. Who were they? *Who were they?* Why did they go off and leave me in the middle of heaven knows where? Did they mean me to die? Or just to be lost?

If they meant me to die, she concluded, they'd have slit my throat and done with it; there was no shilly-shallying with that pair; they'd have done it as soon as kiss your hand; so I reckon they just wanted me away from the train. And now I'm away they don't care a button what happens to me.

But where was Cold Voice going? And why didn't he want the other one along with him?

Suddenly she remembered an odd little passage of dialogue heard in Colonel Clipspeak's office, when they were trying to make contact with the Leicester Square Headquarters by means of the electric kettle and the colonel's dress sabre.

"Unloose the tempest."

"Master, it shall be done."

I do believe that was the self-same voice, Sauna thought. It had that same icy-cold twang, brings you out in goose pimples just to think of it. And the other one, the whiny one asking and begging and asking—why did that seem someway familiar too? Who does it sound like? Someone I haven't known very long?

The Mayor of Newcastle?

No.

It was Tom Flint, she thought suddenly. Of course, it was Tom Flint.

The discovery was not cheering. In fact it was very lowering. Sauna turned for relief to Dr. Wren's remedy for overcoming depression and boredom: the use of figures.

"The multiplication table has helped me out of many a tight corner," he told her. "And out of some loose corners too!"

Oh, Dr. Wren, thought Sauna, how I wish you were here now. I don't know what kind of a corner I'm in, but it feels dead uncomfortable. Nine nines are eighty-one, nine tens are ninety. Nine elevens are ninety-nine, nine twelves are—

The track narrowed here, between steep mossy banks, and the surface underfoot became a gluey mixture of snow and deep mud; sometimes she sank up to her knees; she lost a shoe and barely managed to rescue it by delving down in freezing mud with her hands, then lost the other one altogether. Only the knowledge that it would be wholly impossible to battle a way through that fallen tree kept her from turning back.

But what if this path leads nowhere, comes to a stop? she thought.

Then I'm really done.

But a path has to lead *somewhere*, doesn't it?

She struggled on. Eight eights are sixty-four, eight nines are seventy-two.

After a while the path widened again, and the surface improved; now it was firm rock or frozen earth under layers of fallen leaves and snow. Sauna, wincing as she walked on bare and burning feet, remembered an old rhyme that her mother

used to sing about souls after death making their arduous way
through purgatory and its trials.

> If hosen or shoon thou ne'er gavest nane
> The whins shall prick thee to the bare bane.

That old ballad that Mam used to sing. Mam was Scot-
tish, of course. She knew all those old rhymes.
How did the refrain go?

> This ae night, this ae night,
> Every night and alle,
> Fire and sleet and candlelight
> And Heaven receive thy soul . . .

I just wish I could see a bit of fire, a bit of candlelight.
She came round a clump of trees, and found herself in a
clearing. An *assart*. She remembered Dr. Wren explaining the
word one day when the *Cockatrice Belle* was running through
woodland and came to an open space.

"It is a strip of land in the middle of woodland, my child,
which has been opened out, the trees felled and uprooted so
that the ground can be cultivated and crops grown. And
mostly there will be a house, probably the dwelling of the first
farmer who reclaimed the land; often the house may be very
old. Assarts are old, hundreds of years old, from when the
whole country was covered by forest; these days folk do not
choose to live in woodland glades."

There was a house in the clearing.

Oh, Dr. Wren, how I wish you were here.

Dr. Wren had also told them stories in between periods
of instruction. "People need stories," he said to Dakin and

Sauna, "to remind them that reality is not only what we can see or smell or touch. Reality is in as many layers as the globe we live on itself, going inwards to a central core of red-hot mystery, and outwards to unguessable space. People's minds need detaching, every now and then, from the plain necessities of daily life. People need to be reminded of these other dimensions above us and below us. Stories do that."

So he told his stories, which were always startling and often beautiful. The strange, the really strange thing about them was that like dreams they vanished. The very moment after the final sentence was spoken the listeners would find that the whole web of the story had melted from memory, however hard they tried and struggled to hang on to even a single thread.

They complained about this to Dr. Wren, and asked why it should be so.

"We can remember other stories—like Alfred and the Cakes or Bluebeard. So why not yours?"

He laughed and said, "Mine are intended to be lost. And none the worse for that. They are supposed to sink out of view, deep down to where they will do the most good."

If only I could remember one of those stories now, thought Sauna. Just the smallest scrap of one.

But it was no use; she could not. Even the attempt was some help though. It seemed to brace her mind against the sight that she was expecting.

Nine twelves are a hundred and—a hundred and—

The house was very small, stone-built, with a thatched roof. It stood at the opposite end of the clearing. If there had ever been any crop grown in this woodland place, its harvest had long ago been reaped. Snow lay level and untrodden over the sloping ground. Nobody had walked this way for many hours.

But in one of the windows of the house—it had two, both at ground-floor level—there was, unmistakably, a light. The dimnest, smokiest blink, yet a light.

Sauna limped on. What else could she do? There was no possibility of going back. And so far as she could make out the track led on no further than this clearing. Behind the cottage the hill rose steeply. And if there had been a track she could not have followed it. She had come to the end of her strength. She felt unbelievably weary, hollow with hunger, sick with cold. Only this extremity of need drove her on.

For as she neared the cottage, her unexpressed terror was confirmed—one, she now realized, that had been lurking at the back of her mind for the last few hours.

A dark shape stood outside the door—a thing, an effigy of a person, not a real person but a grotesque figure made out of wicker or willow wands. Dozens of wands were loosely, lavishly coiled round to make a bulbous, huge head; masses more sprang from the neck and ran down bulging out into a grotesque body; wands from the shoulders were buckled in at the wrists and spread out again as fingers, curved into a clutching gesture.

Sauna stood still in a numbness of horror. For here was the cottage, here was the figure of her dream.

Then a comforting thought came to her. Perhaps this is all of a dream—the longest, worst dream I have ever dreamed, but still no more than that.

I had better go into the house. Perhaps that will cause me to wake.

Mustering up all her courage, she walked up to the motionless figure, walked past it and knocked on the door. Nobody answered, so she lifted the latch and went in.

Chapter seven

The *Cockatrice Belle* crept along very slowly and mournfully in the days following the loss of Sauna. When they were still at Falstone, Lieutenant Up- fold had had the sensible idea of giving the dog Uli Sauna's skipping-rope and ordering him to follow her track.

This worked well so long as the road ran beside the rail- way, but at Hawick the track of the coach carrying the kid- napped girl diverged from the rail turning north-eastwards, while the train was obliged to continue straight on in a northerly direction.

"Should we send a separate party of men along the road to follow the scent?" worried the colonel. "There aren't many monsters about just now."

"On the whole I think it will be best to keep all our forces together," advised Dr. Wren. "Remember what happened at Willoughby. The lack of monsters may mean they are massing elsewhere. Besides, we may pick up the track at Peebles."

Not happy about this, but as there really seemed no alternative, the colonel accepted Dr. Wren's counsel. He was extremely put out though before they reached Peebles, when the archbishop insisted on a visit to Melrose, which took half a day.

"What in the world is *that* for?" demanded Clipspeak sourly.

"I need to consult the library there," was Dr. Wren's calm answer.

When the archbishop returned to the train, the colonel was pacing to and from, on indignant watch for him.

"Well?" he snapped. "Did you find what you hoped for in the library, may I ask? It's as well there are so few monsters about! Your little side-trip might have cost us dearly!"

"I fear they must be massing farther on. No," said Dr. Wren, "I hardly hoped to find anything. But it was needful to check."

"To check *what?* What, pray, were you looking for?"

"Michael Scott's last book."

"That feller that wrote *Tom Cringle's Log?*"

"No, Colonel, no, no," said the archbishop patiently. "The other one. The thirteenth-century alchemist. As I believe I told you, his grave is in Melrose Abbey, and he is said to have stipulated that his last book, his greatest achievement, should be buried along with him."

"So? Well? Well? Was the book in the grave? Or the municipal library?"

"No, it was in neither of those places. The grave had been opened some time during the last century, but only a single page of manuscript was discovered in it. That *had* been deposited in the municipal library, but it seems that, just last year, it was stolen."

"Disgraceful," remarked the colonel, not particularly interested. "Even public libraries ain't safe from vandals these days. So you had a wasted visit, when we might have been on our way."

"Oh, not entirely wasted," said Dr. Wren peacefully. "Knowledge is always useful. I had a description of the man who stole the page."

At Peebles there was still a somewhat unnerving shortage of monsters. But here the intelligent hound Uli once more picked up the scent of the coach that had carried off Sauna. The trail, not surprisingly, led northwards towards Edinburgh; but then, to the colonel's surprise, it turned west once more, avoiding the main line to Edinburgh and seemed to be heading for Linlithgow and Falkirk.

"Just as I expected," said Dr. Wren with satisfaction. "They are making for the Crook of Devon. A most unchancy place of evil fame and bad repute."

"Then why the plague don't they go across the Forth Bridge and turn left?" demanded the colonel.

"Ah well, there are some natures, Colonel, who strongly dislike crossing running water, specially in wide channels, and will go out of their way to avoid it."

The train suddenly jerked to a halt.

Bellswinger's voice came over the intercom.

"Basilisk attack, sir."

"Are the men at action stations?"

"Yessir."

Colonel Clipspeak hurried off to the observation platform, from which the sky looked like Guy Fawkes being celebrated on *Le Quatorze Juillet*, as the flaming Basilisks hurtled in to attack, and then bore off again into the darkness with the agility of gulls and the ferocity of eagles. Luckily the Cockatrice Corps had picked up a number of tips in

Basilisk warfare as they travelled through the Border Country; this bleak, hilly territory, once ravaged by border raiders, was now the perching place for aerial predators and the natives had learned various canny ways of confronting them. Or, rather, con*backing* them.

"Ye should never, never face a Basilisk heid on," an aged Ettrick shepherd instructed Bellswinger. "They are like the Mirkindoles in that respect. Ye should aye gang at him tersyversy. Shoot at the fearsome beast over your shoulder."

"But suppose that two come at you, from opposite directions, at the same time?"

"Och, ye'll juist hae tae deal wi' them in a parabolical manner."

Lieutenant Upfold, who had cousins in Australia and had visited that land, partly solved this problem by constructing boomerang-rockets, fired by curving projectile pistols. These missiles, flying round in circles, achieved considerable damage among flocks of Basilisks, and were by far the best weapons yet devised for dealing with the unpleasant antagonists.

During the current attack, when the Basilisks were flying low and keeping in close formation, the boomerang-rockets had marked success, knocking down at least seventy-five per cent of the attacking force, and causing the rest to sheer off south-westwards and take refuge in the Pentland Hills.

The train had to halt while the battle raged. A protective screen had to be lowered over the windshield, and it took time to lower and then raise it again. When calm finally succeeded the crackle of pistol-fire and the menacing shrieks, hisses and whistles of the Basilisks, the colonel gave the order to get under way without delay. But while wind-power was still being mustered, a desolate cry from alongside the track caused Sergeant Bellswinger to hesitate.

"Beg pardon, Colonel, sir, but—was that a call for assistance?"

"Help me—oh, please, help me! Help! *Help!*"

"Can it be one of our men, snatched off by a Basilisk?" asked the colonel, frowning. "Light a flare, if you please, Sergeant."

In the greenish light of the flare, they saw a man feebly crawling up the embankment towards the track. He was covered in mud.

"I don't think it's one of ours, sir," said the sergeant. "All ours are accounted for. No serious casualties this time, I'm happy to say. But this fellow looks to be in a poor way. Something about the cut of his jib seems familiar. Clinch and Mollisk, go down and give him a hand."

The injured man seemed unable to walk. He had to be carried.

A ferocious growl from Uli, the Gridelin hound, could be heard as the sufferer was carried aboard, which soon gave a clue as to his identity.

"Good gracious, sir," said Sergeant Bellswinger. "Why, it's our bad penny turned up again. It's Tom Flint."

Sauna's feeling of utter terror, as she lifted the latch of the cottage door and walked in, was not at all diminished by the smell that met her from the interior. It was quite disgusting: sour, stuffy, a mix of dirty, decaying food, and something sweetish and chemical which reminded her of the flat in Manchester. An *armpit* kind of smell, she thought, peering ahead, trying to think how Dr. Wren would have described it. The sort of stuff that people smear over themselves or pour down a drain to try and drown something horrible that's underneath.

The interior was almost entirely dark to anyone coming from out of doors, so she stood still for a moment, until her eyes grew more accustomed. On her left there was a dim glow, and a mild warmth at floor level, and a faint scent, one of the better components of the engulfing odour of the house. This was familiar, and took Sauna back to those summer holidays with Mam and Dad—it was the smell of a peat fire.

"Hallo?" she said hoarsely. The effort it took to open her mouth and speak was enormous. "Is—is anybody here?"

And the answer she received shocked her so badly that her legs almost gave way beneath her.

"*Sauna? Is that my little Sauna?*"

It was the voice she had heard twice on the train: the faint, shrill, wailing travesty of Auntie Floss's voice.

Now, at the far end of the room, she began to make out the shape of a daybed or cot; and on this somebody, some person, was lying, wrapped in shadowy draperies and coverings.

When Sauna, sick with fright and dislike, stepped nearer, she saw twin sparks of light—*eyes*—fixed on her.

"Is—is—*can* that be you, Aunt Florence?" she managed to say.

The person on the couch giggled—an eerie, wholly unexpected sound. It seemed as if not one but several people had all laughed together.

"Who else would it be, dearie? So you got here at last! And a precious long time it took you! And your poor Auntie Flo waiting here for you, so patiently—so-o-o patiently. What kept you?"

"Well—I—"

"It wasn't nice of you—no, it wasn't—to stay away such a long, long time when your auntie wanted you so bad—your auntie that took you into her own place and was always so kind . . ."

"Aunt Florence," said Sauna desperately. "How did you ever *get* here?"

This was a daft conversation. How could that—that thing on the bed be her Aunt Florence? She could still see nothing more than a shadowy shape with twin points of pale light set close together at one end.

"How did I get here, dearie? Why, my—my friends brought me."

"From the flat? From Brylcreme Court? From Manchester?"

"Of course!" sang out the voice, much amused, and again it was as if not one but several voices all spoke together. "My friends brought me!"

Friends! thought Sauna. But Aunt Florence never had any friends. Nobody ever came to her flat except for readings. And she never went out to play whist or bingo, or to coffee-mornings. There were no friends. Aunt Floss used to talk to herself. Or to the kettle, in that spooky way. Never to neighbours.

"But didn't they bring *you*, lovey?" the shrill voice persisted. "My friends? Didn't they bring you here? Where are they now? Why don't they come in? They know, they know how much I want to see them again?"

"Who?"

"My friends, my friends!" whined the voice, and ran up to a hysterical scream. "Why won't they come in?"

Sauna thought about the pair who had driven her in the carriage. If there *were* two of them.

"Two men fetched me—" she began cautiously.

"Where are they now?"

Sauna began to shiver.

"I don't know. They threw me out of the carriage. It turned and drove off, I suppose. And—and a tree fell—you can't go back that way now—"

"Oh-oh-oh!" the voice wailed. "*Why* wouldn't they stay? Friends ought to stay together."

There was something horribly *wrong* about the voice—about the figure and shape altogether—as if some foreigner with only the vaguest conception of what Aunt Florence had been like were trying to act the part of Florence in a play written by somebody else who had never seen her. Sauna began to think she might easily go stark-staring mad herself if she did not instantly take some sensible, practical action. By now her eyes were accustomed to the gloom in the room. Apart from the truckle-bed there was no furniture, save a couple of stools by the fireside and a large cardboard carton under the window.

Sauna moved to the fire, blew on it, and laid on another hunk of peat from a pile she found heaped against the wall.

"I'm cold and hungry, Aunt Florence," she said as matter-of-factly as she could manage. "Is there anything to eat?"

"Food in the box. Food in the box. Food in the box." The answer came in a toneless gabble, as if from a machine.

A small flare of light from the new lump of peat on the fire revealed that the box was sealed shut with parcel-tape, had never been opened.

"Are there any tools here: scissors, knives, forks?"

"Tools? I don't know what you mean—"

Sauna wondered if the sort of things she needed might be found in the back room. A doorway at the foot of the bed opened on to darkness. For various reasons she felt very reluctant to walk on into that black place. Something in the other room seemed to be rustling . . . She would just as soon not know what it was.

She approached the carton, delving rather hopelessly in her pockets as she did so for anything—a paper-clip, bent pin, hair-grip, rusty nail—that might help to slit through the thick tape. The first thing her fingers encountered was a tangle of rope, the rope that had tied her wrists. Under that was something unfamiliar and with an odd, complicated shape. What could it be? Withdrawing her hand she realized that what she held was the pair of tiny dolls, fastened together by the outsize kilt-pin.

She had left the dolls on the shelf over Mrs. Churt's kitchen range, and after they were dry she had picked them up and put them in her pocket. That was when she and Dakin were running to and fro, carrying out trays of blackberry tea to the men on the line.

Well, the dolls were quite dry now. Carefully, Sauna pulled out the pin. Its point would be just the thing to score through the sticky tape.

From the bed at the end of the room came a hoarse gasp. "Oh! the pain, the pain! What are you doing?"

"Opening the box," replied Sauna, scoring the point of the pin across the tape and prising up the flaps.

The box proved to be full of paper-wrapped bags and packets, jammed solidly close together. Some felt like flour, or cheese, or macaroni. Others like raisins or biscuits. There were tins and jars as well. All right, so long as there's a tin-opener somewhere, thought Sauna.

With the point of the pin she tore open a packet of biscuits and nibbled one. It tasted of ginger. Faintly, distantly, as if from another life she remembered that her Aunt Flo-

rence had been very fond of ginger biscuits and always had a
couple of packets in the flat.

"Would you like a ginger biscuit, Aunt Florence?"

"Oh!" cried the sharp thin voice. "How can you offer me
food to eat when I suffer such pain? I can't eat—I can't eat—
never any more—I am far too ill."

"Do you want a drink?"

Though dear knows where I'll find one, thought Sauna.

"Drink. Drink. *Thirst* . . . Mug on floor . . ."

Overcoming her extreme distaste, Sauna approached the
bed (where the smell was even more powerful, thick, like
mephitic gas) and found a clumsy china mug on the ground.

"Water barrel by door."

Sauna remembered with horror that grotesque, spooky
figure, all made of willow wands, standing just outside the
cottage door. Was it still there? Or had it got up and walked
silently away, once Sauna had passed by?

But the water barrel proved to be inside the door, not outside. She dipped out a mugful of water and took it back to
the figure on the bed, who received it in two hands skinny as
bunches of twigs—skinny as that creature's hands.

The cup was raised, but Aunt Florence (if it was she) did
not drink. Instead two brilliant pale eyes stared at Sauna over
the rim of the mug. The face behind the mug was still in
shadow.

"So long to wait. Waiting. Wanting. In cold, in dark."

The whisper was like the telephone message in Colonel
Clipspeak's office. It echoed from all around, from the walls,
the ceiling, the floor. Like a rustle of snakes uncoiling.

Sauna said desperately, "Who *are* you? You are not really my Aunt Florence, are you? Who are you really?"

The hands opened and let the china mug crash to the floor.

"I am the Queen, Hel. Hela. The Queen of Air and Darkness. All the powers of the air are my servants."

Then the figure lay flat back on the bed—like a cardhouse that has fallen down—and neither spoke nor moved any more.

Sauna fled to the door, opened it and ran outside.

But by now the blizzard had risen to full force; a gust of sleet lashed her in the face like a cat-o'-nine tails, the force of the wind made her stagger. Despairingly she realized that she had not the remotest chance of surviving a journey of unknown length and direction, shoeless, through strange woods and mountains, in such weather.

But the alternative—a night passed in that gruesome little house . . . with that grisly, mummy-like replica of Aunt Florence—how could she possibly endure it?

I've *got* to endure it, thought Sauna slowly. Remember those chaps on the *Cockatrice Belle*—remember what they've got to put up with. Snarks, Kelpies, Basilisks, Trolls. They never even know what's coming next. If they can keep going, I can too.

Squaring her shoulders, she walked back into the house and piled another handful of peat-lumps on the fire. Then she helped herself to a few more ginger biscuits and munched them slowly. The smell in the house had killed her hunger, but she knew it was important to eat something. The mug had smashed, but she still had one shoe. She filled it out of the barrel and drank a few mouthfuls of stale-tasting water from the heel.

Then, pulling the kilt-pin from her pocket, she sat down beside the fire with her back against the wall, clutching the pin in her right hand. She had no other weapon; and it was better than nothing.

After a while her left hand stole back to her pocket and

came out with the two dolls. I'm glad I found them, she thought drowsily. They were part of the old life with Mam and Dad. Perhaps they'll bring me luck. Dr. Wren said something about them. He told a story . . . what was it?

Her head drooped forward on to her knees. She slept.

Chapter eight

As soon as **Tom Flint** had been dragged on board, the *Cockatrice Belle* shot off again at top speed. They were now running along the coastal plain, where the Forth narrows from firth to river; the track was in better condition here than in the hilly country they had left, and this was an advantage as the principal adversaries in this region were the slow-moving Kelpies, who unless they climbed up on to the rails, had little chance of doing much damage. To prevent their invading the way ahead of the train, Major Scanty had evolved a stellar-powered ray-dart which proved an excellent deterrent; it did not kill, but shocked and winded them, so that they scrambled back off the embankment, wailing with rage and distaste.

"All very well, Scanty, *in its way*," grumbled the colonel, "but our job is to get rid of the brutes once and for all, not just give 'em a twinge in their backsides."

"Our task, as I understand it, Colonel," said Scanty mildly, "is to proceed northwards to the neighbourhood of the Kingdom of Fife at all possible speed, and there to await orders as to the general conduct of the campaign."

"Hmn, well, yes, that's so, certainly. But what I ask myself is, supposin' we get there and can't make contact with Gladiolus, *then* what?"

During the last week it had proved impossible to get through to army headquarters in Leicester Square.

"If only we hadn't mislaid that gal!" fretted the colonel. "What a crass bit of mismanagement *that* was!"

"It certainly was," sighed the archbishop. "But still I have not lost hope of picking up the trail of her abductors. We must not despair."

Indeed they did pick up the trail at Falkirk, but lost it again directly.

The battle with the Basilisks at Linlithgow had caused a good deal of structural damage to the train's roof and windows. The colonel decreed that repairs were to be carried out while the train was in motion; there was no time to be lost. All the crew were at work—the men were just as anxious as the officers to rescue Sauna.

Meanwhile the care of Tom Flint was left to Mrs. Churt and Dakin; principally to Dakin.

The injured man had been taken to a tiny cabin directly behind the engine. It was hot, noisy, and cramped. Brag and Minch, the two men who first occupied it, had moved out and taken over the quarters of Forby and Wintless, who had been killed in a night skirmish with Trolls outside Newcastle.

The cabin was so hot and airless that nobody wanted it.

Dakin was in very low spirits, touchy, miserable, and forlorn. He missed Sauna all the time, and was desperately worried about her; what could be happening to her? Where had she been taken? Was she still alive, even?

He felt very badly about not having been able to prevent her abduction. Though it was not his fault—the birds had prevented him—he felt that people who were not on the scene must blame him for not having done something more active, or yelled for help sooner.

He went about his duties glumly and talked to nobody, not realizing how many people felt sorry for him.

And—worse than all the rest—the Gridelin hound, Uli, was in a state of utter dejection. Dakin had always had a notion that Uli loved Sauna best of everyone on the train; now he was sure. The great hound crept mournfully about with ears and tail dangling so low that they swept the ground, collecting dust; he ate next to nothing, whined outside the door of Sauna's cabin, and lay for hours with his chin resting on her skipping-rope. Only at Hawick, Peebles, and Falkirk, where it was momentarily possible to pick up the scent of her abductors, did he show any signs of life or interest. He did, it was true, growl furiously when Tom Flint was brought on board at Linlithgow, and outside the door of his sick-bay if he chanced to pass it, but this animosity never lasted long; he returned miserably to the galley and lay on Mrs. Churt's cross-stitch, getting horribly in her way.

"What's the matter with that fellow Flint, anyway?" she asked, giving Dakin a cup of hot wintergreen tea for the sick man. "I never *did* fancy that feller above half—why does Dr. Wren say he mustn't be left alone? A skimpy stick of liquorice in britches, he is, if you ask me! And he hasn't been bit by a Basilisk or anything, has he?"

"No, it's mighty queer," said Dakin. "He's not wounded—or even much bruised—but he's very weak, delirious, I think. He says his hands and feet hurt terribly, and his face—could it be frostbite? He keeps on all the time, mumbling about hands and feet and faces. I can't make head or tail of what he says, or what's really the matter with him."

"He say anything about where he was? When he was off the train?"

"Nothing that makes sense."

"Or about Sauna? After all, he went missing the same time she did."

Dakin shook his head.

"Well, you better take him this drink while it's hot," said Mrs. Churt crossly. "I can tell you, I need five pair of hands round this galley. I wish Sauna was here, and that's a fact."

Chafed and annoyed, though he could not exactly have said with whom, Dakin returned to the noisy dark cabin squashed in behind the engine. Here Tom Flint was tossing and turning on his narrow bunk.

"Don't leave me!" he cried out wildly. "Why did you leave me?"

"Well, it wasn't for very long!" snapped Dakin. "Here, drink this blessed stuff and stop kicking up such a row."

But Tom Flint spilled most of the wintergreen.

"Oh!" he cried. "See the people with their faces all on fire! Oh, look at them! Look at them! And their hands and feet burning like torches! How terrible upon the mountains are the feet of those—of those—"

He kicked off the covers and stared wildly at his own feet. "I think they are growing webs. I will thrust my hands and feet into the flame," he told Dakin.

"I wish you'd stow your gab," said Dakin.

Dr. Wren came along to visit the patient. Before becoming an archbishop he had trained in medicine, and so had been very busy caring for all the men injured in the Basilisk attack.

He felt Flint's forehead and hands, then stared into his eyes.

"It's odd. He doesn't have a fever, although he's so hot and restless; but just look at his eyes."

"What's up with 'em?" asked Dakin.

"The pupils are pinpoints—as if he'd been staring at a bright light."

"Not in here he hasn't," said Dakin.

"Well, give him one of these mushroom tablets—if you can get him calm enough to swallow it. And you must stay with him. I don't want him left, not for more than a moment or so. I'll be back as soon as I can."

Why should *I* get saddled with this boring job? thought Dakin resentfully, as Dr. Wren bustled off to care for his wounded men.

"Here, swallow this pill, will you, and stop moaning," Dakin snapped, as Flint heaved himself about, and by luck more than dexterity managed to get it down the patient's throat. After a while, Flint calmed down a trifle.

He glanced warily round the tiny room.

"They went off and left me," he told Dakin. "They *betrayed* me. After all their promises."

"Who did?"

"Never you mind!" whispered Flint. His eyes slid sideways and met those of Dakin. He smiled. "Do you want to know where the girl is?" he said. "Do you want to know *why* they took her?"

He pulled a crumpled sheet of paper out of his pocket. "They forgot I have this." Now his smile was sly and triumphant. "They left me—so why should I care for them?"

Dakin was not at all interested in the piece of paper. He

said angrily, "Was it *you* who helped snatch Sauna? Was it? Do you know where she is? Tell me!"

Tom Flint was staring at the paper. "If only I could read it . . ." he muttered irritably. "Here—you try!" He pushed the sheet at Dakin, who gave it a cursory glance.

"No, I can't read it," he said shortly. "It doesn't make sense. It's in some crazy writing—nothing but noughts and crosses. Tell me about Sauna. *Where did they take her?*"

"Up towards Crook of Devon—up towards Rumbling Bridge," whispered Flint. "That's where the witches are. Oh yes! There's always been covens in places like that—dark places, deep places, where the water comes crashing and sliding down, where the woods pull in till it's dark at midday. The girl's grandfather, he was a warlock, and her great-grandfather too—all the way back, *all* the way back to Grandfather Cain! *I* know! I've been there too!"

"Is that where Sauna was taken? Crook of Devon?" persisted Dakin. "Who by? Where is it?"

"You see," said Tom Flint, "they need hands. *Human* hands. To do their jobs." He spread out his own hands, then bundled them under his armpits with a childish wail. "They are burning! Burning like phosphorus! All—all the waters of paradise will not quench that fire!"

"Tell me why they took Sauna?" Dakin repeated.

"They need the girl to find the book. Human hands," cried Flint. "They need hands. They can't—you see—dig it out." He grinned maliciously. "And the girl—with her gift—is as good as a truffle-hound."

"*Where is she?*"

"Sorrow," said Flint. "They shall eat the bread of sorrow and burn in perpetual fire."

"I wish you would talk sense. Did you or did you not go with those men who took Sauna?"

"How can I tell?" said Flint. "After all, they may still come back for me. I daren't risk it."

"Risk what? Oh!" cried Dakin furiously. "You are hopeless!"

"Yes, hopeless. Hopeless, hopeless. With hands and feet and face of fire."

The loud wail of the monster-alarm echoed up and down the train. Dakin jumped up impatiently and left the cabin, slamming the door behind him. "Off you go!" Flint shouted after him. "Don't let the sergeant forget to unwrap his lucky parcel."

Surely nothing can happen to the fellow in there, thought Dakin, running to his own quarters and grabbing his goggles and electric crossbow. He had no idea what Flint's last remark could have meant—just rubbish, most probably.

But when the alert was over—it proved to have been a mistaken warning, a group of red deer crossing the track—and Dakin returned to the cabin, Tom Flint seemed to have undergone a surprising change. His cheeks were plumper, he was a better colour, he talked more sensibly. If he were a balloon, thought Dakin, I'd say somebody had blown him up.

"You see, the ozone layer was punctured," he suddenly remarked confidentially to Dakin. "That's how all the monsters got in. It happens easily during the Sleep of Reason."

"Oh?" said Dakin, neither understanding nor believing him. "Who punctured it, then?"

"Fumes . . . heat . . . all these products of a more comfortable life. But of course my friends were lightning-quick to take advantage of the situation." Flint spoke proudly, like the managing director of a company giving a successful annual report. "They slipped the monsters through."

"But why? from where?"

"Oh . . . somewhere else . . ."

"Why?" Dakin asked again.

"To produce maximum chaos, in order to take over the globe. This is the weakest point, so this is where they began. Naturally. Disintegration of the human ethos. It's like . . ." Tom Flint's eyes wandered round the stuffy little cabin. For a moment, disconcertingly, the irises disappeared clean out of sight, leaving only the whites. "It is like growing a bacterial culture," he said then, his eyes returning to normal. "You need some really dirty, scummy water. Nourishment for the new organism you want to grow."

"What organism?" Dakin yawned. He was bored. The little cabin had no windows; he wished he could walk along the corridor and see where the train had got to.

"My friends. The adversaries."

"Adversaries of what?"

"Honour. Order. Respect for law. What my friends really want to get hold of is Scott's book. The *Book of Power.* For their task must be done by human hands," he repeated. "And this is where you can help them—"

Dakin yawned again. He did not want to help anybody. He was fed up with standing on the sidelines, being helpful. What he wanted was glory, to be in a battle again, rattling on his drum, feeling important and powerful, part of it all.

He remembered the terrific excitement of the battle at Manchester. Lost in recall, he paid little heed to the voice of Tom Flint, who was waffling on about this old book that had been lodged in a hermit's cell hundreds of years ago. "Sorrow—not in the sense of grief, you understand, but from the old word *sorren,* meaning a service of hospitality to a clan chieftain . . ."

Oh, blow you and your sorrows, thought Dakin, wishing there might be another Kelpie warning. Kelpies were slow beasts; they didn't provide the mad excitement of Basilisks, or the terror of Trolls or Griffins, but anything would be better than being obliged to sit here and listen to this interminable dreary rubbish about abbeys and caves and glens.

"What was your favourite food when you were small?" Tom Flint unexpectedly asked.

"Oh!" Dakin was startled. "I suppose, Pollylollies. Oh, I could have eaten hundreds of them when I was a kid—"

Gorgeously coloured, they were. Came in little string sacks.

"Suppose you had a hundred tons of them now?"

"Yuk!"

"Well, what would you like best in the world *now?* A helibike?"

"What would be the good? Too many monsters about."

He had longed for one, though. Only the sons of millionares could afford them, or gangsters.

"What then?" the insidious voice kept pressing. "What would you really, really like best?"

"Just playing on my drum," Dakin croaked. "In a battle. That's what I like best."

"Ah . . ."

The alarm sounded again. Dakin dashed gladly to the door.

"We shall see what we can do," Tom Flint called after him. "Don't forget the book. Don't forget it! It will be wrapped in cloth-of-copper. Pinned with a gold pin. It would be best if you found it before your cousin Sauna does . . . otherwise the glory will be hers, of course, not yours . . ."

Oh be quiet, you, Dakin thought, I'm not listening. And he ran on, even when a curious shriek sounded from the cabin behind him—a shriek of pain, was it, or joy?

The train had come to a halt because the lights of Alloa

were visible across the estuary; but there were Kelpies ahead, ensconced in large numbers on the viaduct.

After the long, arduous and tiresome battle which followed—no drumwork was required, only dogged bashing and close combat with electric rays—Dakin was hurt, and suffered from a sharp sense of injustice when the colonel, spotting him, sharply ordered him to get back to Flint's cabin, on the double.

"You should not have left it. Why did you do so? You were not supposed to quit your watch. The archbishop was most emphatic that he should not be left alone."

"But I wanted to help fight the Kelpies, sir." Dakin was injured and virtuous. "It was battle stations."

"There were enough men for that without you. Return to your post at once."

And, disastrously, when Dakin got back to the cabin, Tom Flint was not there.

"Perhaps he jumped off the observation platform?" suggested Major Scanty.

"Impossible!" declared the colonel. "I was there all the time. It is extremely vexatious. What do you think can have happened to him, Archbishop?"

"I am afraid his friends may have come back for him."

"And who's been rummaging in my bunk?" demanded Sergeant Bellswinger furiously.

"Somebody after your secret parcel, Ser'nt?" teased Ensign Pomfret.

Everybody knew that, ever since the train had left Manchester, the sergeant had a mysterious flat packet, done up in snark-proof, waterproof paper, which he tucked into his battle-blouse before every engagement. No one had asked what it was. Many had guessed.

"Ah, no, that's safe enough." The sergeant tapped his diaphragm. "But I'd like to know what so-and-so's been fossicking in my berth. I bet it *was* that mealy-mouthed supercargo. Everyone else was out fighting except for Mrs. Churt, and I'm sure it wasn't her."

Dakin was in slight disgrace.

Chapter nine

Daylight of a sort had returned to the cottage when Sauna next woke.

The storm still raged outside. She could see a grey whirl of snow pass the window. When she opened the door snowflakes slashed at her like razor-blades.

She flinched back inside again and shut the door. The fire glowed faintly; with blue fingers she piled on more lumps of peat then, for the first time, forced herself to look around the small, frowsty room.

The floor of beaten earth was piled several inches deep with layers of newspaper, yellow and crinkled with age and dirt. The last date was ten years back. When Mam and Dad were still alive, thought Sauna sadly.

Then she compelled herself to look at the narrow cot-bed which stood by the wall opposite the entrance door. Something lay on it covered and wrapped in thin moth-eaten grey blankets, stiff with dirt. Something faintly moved. Sauna could see—*just*—the weak, flickering rise and fall of breath. Holding her own breath, battling against violent repugnance, she tiptoed over and stared at what lay there.

It seemed more like a skeleton than a human being. Sparse yellow hair spread thinly over the bony scalp. The face was skin stretched tight over bone: greyish skin, speckled and blotched and wrinkled and scabbed—more like something you'd find out of doors than a person, thought Sauna; fungus, a rotten log, a withered cabbage leaf. The eye-sockets were sunken in shrunken knot-holes like tree bark. The hands, lying loose on the pillow, were gnarled like roots.

Don't wake. *Please* don't wake, thought Sauna. She crept away from the bed, still holding her breath, although the howl of the wind outside drowned any noise made inside the house, save the buzz of several large bluebottle flies, which slammed angrily from side to side, up under the ceiling.

What I need, thought Sauna rather hopelessly, is a pot, something to heat water in.

She tiptoed into the back room. It was divided from the front by a short passage, only half a dozen steps long. In the middle of this a ladder fastened to the wall led up to a square opening, presumably giving on to a loft.

Sauna might have thought she was now immune to shocks, but the back room startled her so much that she had to lean against the door frame to get her breath. For—apart from a dresser along the opposite wall—the room was a faithful replica of her Aunt Florence's front parlour in the flat in Manchester. Here was the table with its discoloured lace cloth, here the red velour-covered chairs, the television set, the tiled fireplace with a paper fan in a jam jar, the potted palm and, covering every horizontal surface, the myriads of little china mugs and vases, each with its message: "A Present from Southsea," "A Present from Westcliffe," "A Present from Hove," "A Present from Margate," "A Present from St. Leonards-on-Sea."

The sight of the back room was so staggering that Sauna had to lean against the wall till her legs recovered their strength. She stared at what she saw for a long minute, almost stupefied with disbelief. They can't be here. They just can't. How can they?

Then—*is* that Aunt Florence, after all?

If not, who else can it be?

Noting an old enamel milkpan and a battered spoon and fork on the dresser, she mechanically picked up these articles and returned to the front room.

There she had her second shock in five minutes, quite as bad as the first one. For the figure on the bed was now sitting bolt upright, grinning at her with eyes turned to slits.

"Getting settled in? That's right," remarked the high, lilting voice. "Make a little porridge, why don't you? Aye, parritch, parritch—a gude Scots dish!" And the creature giggled, showing two rows of yellow artificial teeth.

"*Are* you Aunt Florence?"

"Who else should I be, dearie? Or else I'll do till the next one comes along." Another giggle. "But I told you. I am the Queen of Air and Darkness. All the powers of the air are my friends. Astarte, Abiron, Asmodeus, Belial, Buktanoos, Baal, Chemosh, Dusien, Eblis, Musboot, Zulbazan . . . all, all my friends. And this one, too."

She gave a twitch to her blankets, and—to Sauna's horror—a grey head poked out from under them: that of a large, flea-bitten, seedy-looking rat, which peered watchfully at Sauna, showed its teeth, then let out a shrill, thin, hostile sound between a hiss and a squeak.

"*Oh no!*" Sauna clutched her pan by the handle, raised it

up instinctively—she detested rats—but the voice from the bed halted her.

"Don't you go for to bash him, dearie. He's my friend. *He* won't hurt *you*, if *you* don't hurt *him*. That is—not unless I tell him."

Aunt Florence grinned again, slit-eyed.

"We find our friends where we can, eh? Don't we, my bubsy, my mutchkin? My precious, my piggesnie? Where we can. Later on, you can see my *other* friends. Yes; later on they'll be back. Now you make that porridge, why don't you? We must keep strong, yes, keep strong. And ratto here would be glad of a nuncheon."

At Alloa the *Cockatrice* crew had a lot of bridge-building to do before the viaduct across the Links of Forth was safe; it took them two days' work, and the nights were passed in battling off hordes of Kelpies who would have undone all the work again.

Alloa was a fishing and ferry town where large boats had once tied up. It lay between three rivers, the Devon, the Black Devon, and the wide Forth itself, meandering in shining links across the marshy plain to meet its estuary. Few people lived here any more, because of the Kelpies, which came in extra numbers because of the double tides. The town was wreathed in juicy green weed and smelt of salt damp. To the north, less than a mile away across the flat floor of the valley, on the other side of the Devon river, rose the menacing slopes of the Ochils, like a steep volcanic wall—which they once had been—clothed in oak and fir, capped with snow.

There was a rumour running about the train that a big

battle was imminent. No one knew where it had started. Everybody was keyed-up and excited.

When Dakin took in the colonel's eleven o'clock acorn coffee (he had been allotted this task since the loss of Sauna) he found a conference going on with Clipspeak, Upfold, Major Scanty, and the archbishop.

"There is a legend, a folk-myth, or whatever you care to call it, current in Melrose that Michael Scott spent some of the last weeks of his life in Sorrow Abbey. And that he may perhaps have left the book there," said Dr. Wren.

"Oh!" exclaimed Dakin, suddenly putting two and two together. "That must have been what old Liquorice was jawing on about—I mean, Tom Flint. Sorrow, he kept saying. Sorrow, Sorrow."

"Flint? He mentioned Sorrow Abbey? What did he say about it?" Dr. Wren was galvanized. "Why, pray, did you not tell us this before?"

"I forgot," mumbled Dakin. "He said such a lot. It didn't seem important. He was going on and on about glens and abbeys and hermits' caves . . ."

"You *forgot!* Wretched boy! Did he mention the location of Sorrow Abbey?"

"Is it not on the map?" suggested Colonel Clipspeak hopefully.

"Unfortunately no, Colonel. It was sacked and pillaged so many times during the Border Wars that its whereabouts now are wholly uncertain. It seems reasonable to assume, however, that it is not too far distant from the town of Dollar (probably Dolour in the first place), and presumably situated somewhere in Glen Sorrow, which runs up from Dollar to the north-east of Ben Cleuch."

"Yes, that makes sense," agreed the colonel, consulting

his wall map. "But if it is not there any longer I do not see that there is much use in sending an expeditionary force to search for this hypothetical volume—if there are not even *ruins*. We can hardly search the whole glen?"

"What else did Tom Flint say to you, boy? Try to rack your brains—this is terribly important."

"The book. He said it was wrapped in cloth of copper. Pinned with a gold pin. What is this book, sir?"

"Michael Scott's *Book of Power*. It is said to answer every possible question—whether moral, scientific, practical, or theoretical."

"A kind of Enquire Within Upon Everything," remarked Upfold. "Pretty handy, hey? Would presumably tell us how to get rid of the monsters."

"What is even *more* important," said Dr. Wren, "is to prevent it falling into the hands of the adversaries."

"Adversaries. That was what Flint called them too," said Dakin. "His friends, he said they were."

"Fine friends! He'll be sorry at the end of the day," snapped Scanty.

"Yes," recalled Dakin. "He wasn't so happy about them when he thought they had skived off and left him, and his hands and feet hurt him so bad. I asked where they had taken Sauna and he said—wait a mo, I'm getting it—something about Crook of Devon and Rumbling Bridge. He said—he said there were lots of witches there."

"Used to be, a couple of centuries ago," said Dr. Wren. "The Ochils have always been borderline country—between lowlands and highlands, between this world and the next. Did Flint say what his friends proposed to do with the *Book of Power*?"

"I've forgotten," said Dakin sadly. "Something to do with

the disintegration of the human ethos. There was a lot of long words."

"Oh, why didn't I stay with the miserable wretch myself?" lamented the archbishop.

"You were saving a good many men's lives who had been severely hurt by Basilisks," the colonel briskly reminded him. "Who would almost certainly be dead by now if it weren't for you."

They all stared at Dakin, as if they would like to pull memory out of him like teeth.

"Maximum chaos," Dakin remembered. "First they got the monsters through a hole in the ozone layer. Now they want to stir up more trouble."

"And the book will help them do this."

"S'pose so."

Dakin felt dreadfully tired. What with watching Tom Flint, and guilty worry over Sauna, and the Kelpie battle, and then feeling that everybody disapproved of him, all he wanted to do was lie down and forget his troubles in sleep. He was aware of the onset of a yawn, working its way up all the way from his toes. He struggled against it until his ears crackled, but out it came.

"All right, boy, you can go," said the colonel wearily.

A croaking voice suddenly made them all jump. It came from nobody in the room. It was faint, as if it floated in from far away, shrill and full of malice.

"Don't go to Dollar!" it said. "Don't go to Dollar!" And then ran off into gabbled nursery nonsense. "A dillar a dollar a ten o'clock scholar, what makes you rise so soon, don't look for Sauna unless you would mourn her, she'll die before the new moon. King Edward's Day, King Edward's Day. That's when they gather, that's when they play. That's when their strength is highest. We must, we must have it by then."

The voice died away.

"That was my Auntie Floss," said Dakin, working his tongue around his mouth to moisten it. "Or, at least, it sounded like her the time I went to her place in Manchester. And I thought I heard Sauna's voice too—just for a moment."

They all stared at him. He suddenly remembered something.

"Tom Flint had this bit of paper. He said his friends forgot he had it. He couldn't read it. Nor could I. I put it in my pocket when the siren went—"

He pulled it out: dirty, crumpled, greasy, slightly frayed at the cracks where it had been folded.

The eyes of everybody in the room fastened on it like staples.

"That's Ogham script," said Dr. Wren.

"Can you read it?" asked the colonel.

Chapter ten

Auntie Floss giggled almost all the time now. She sat with her unbelievably skinny bare legs sticking straight out in front of her on the low bed, and rubbed dark green ointment on to her fingers and toes. Sauna noticed, without any particular increase of disgust, that she had webs between her toes, and there were not so many toes as most people have.

"Always get terrible chilblains this time of year," Floss confided, in the high wheezy voice that sounded like a tape played at double speed. "Wintergreen is best for chilblains. I told them, Put it in the box. In the box, I told them."

The box of groceries might have been packed by a computer. There was powdered tarragon, but no sugar; flour, but no butter; isinglass, but no soap; gum tragacanth, but no mustard; biscuits, but no cheese; washing-soda, but no salt. Tins of corned beef and soup were useless because there was no tin-opener, either in the box or in the cottage. Sauna had managed to cook a potful of porridge over the fire with oatmeal and some water from the barrel (this was full of green slime, but she supposed that boiling would disinfect it). When the blizzard outside died down a little she fetched in a bowlful of snow and left it to melt. And she found an iron bar to poke the fire with, and more peat in a shed.

Seen in daylight the wicker figure outside the door, now thickly covered with snow, looked harmless and inoffensive enough; she supposed that it was simply put there to frighten. Or perhaps as a sign, like a barber's pole: this is the witch's cottage.

"How long have you been here, Aunt Floss?" she tried asking.

The creature on the bed giggled.

"Fifty years, my dearie. Since the newspapers were first put down on the floor. Your grandpa was alive then. I put down those papers. They've lasted well."

"That's just not possible," Sauna said. "Anyway, the papers are only ten years old."

But that was all the answer she got.

Among the contents of the cardboard carton were countless pills, in various little pots and vials and bottles and flasks. Aunt Floss swallowed pills continually in handfuls.

She used to do that in Manchester too, remembered Sauna; that is, if it is Auntie Floss? Or does she just do it to make me believe that she is Auntie Floss?

"When you get to my age and state of health, dearie, your system needs extra vitamins," the creature giggled. "You'll have to start taking them too, by and by. When you take on the job here. It wears you out, that it does!"

"I'm not staying here," Sauna said.

"That's what you think, dearie. You'll feel different later."

When the porridge was cooked, Sauna ate hers out of the saucepan, standing in the open front door, looking at the whirling snow. She had found only one bowl on the dresser, so spooned a helping of porridge into it for the creature on the bed, but could not bear to be a spectator of the eating process. She had a horrible feeling that the oatmeal was in fact eaten by the rat, Maukin, who peered out sometimes from under the covers and bared its teeth evilly at Sauna.

"My mannie," Aunt Floss called it. "My little piggesnie. My ratto."

After midday, when the snow began to slacken off, Aunt Floss said, "We'll tell our fortunes. Now go in the parlour, switch on the TV."

"Are you crazy? There's no current. There's no electricity. No aerial."

Aunt Floss giggled. "*That's* no matter! We managed without it for thousands of years. Switch on, I say."

Shrugging, Sauna went into the back room.

"Mind my china!" came the shrill exhortation. "Mind my precious things!"

Edging between the table with its load of tiny china pots and the wall, Sauna pressed the ON button of the TV set. A light flickered in the middle of the screen.

She suddenly heard Dakin's voice saying, "The book will help them."

Colonel Clipspeak said, "They want to stir up more trouble."

Aunt Floss in the next room cried out, "Don't go to Dollar! Don't go to Dollar! You'll all be killed if you do!" Then she began to sing, a squeaky nursery rhyme.

"Stop that!" shouted Sauna. She pressed the button again. The flickering light faded and vanished.

In the front room the being on the bed propped itself against the wall and sat crosslegged, grinning at Sauna, with slit eyes shining green.

"Plenty of things you don't know yet, my pettikin!"

Sauna walked to the open door and stood breathing huge gulps of air. The cold burned her. But the sky was clear now; no more snow fell. The little glade around the cottage shone with reflected snow-light. Up above, to right and left, the great fir-hung mountains towered like a wall.

The voice from inside called "Come here. Come back, lambskin. There's lot of things that want doing. Things I need!"

With huge reluctance, Sauna turned back into the stinking room. Even though her bare feet were frozen, she had rather stand in the doorway, breathe fresh air, look at the white emptiness and dark forest outside, than walk back into that fetid atmosphere.

The creature on the bed said, "Now, dearie, you have to go out on an errand for me. Up the hill, three turns of the path. Young legs and feet, young hands, you can easily do it. Only three turns of the path. Where the old monks once used to live. You go up there. Fetch it for me."

"I can't fetch anything," Sauna said. "I've only one shoe. I'm not going barefoot in the snow."

There was a pause. The creature in the bed seemed to consider.

Time went by. Then the creature said, "But, pet, your things are in there, in the press. In the back room. Cupboard under the dresser."

"My things? How can they possibly be? I don't believe you."

"Go and look, pettikin."

Sauna looked in the cupboard under the dresser. There

was her shabby blue travel bag, the one she had brought back from Spain. In it was a queer selection of her old clothes and belongings—clothes she had taken to Spain on that holiday, school uniforms from several years back, sweaters that had ravelled to pieces and been thrown away in Newcastle, beach flip-flops, outworn trainers. No winter boots.

"No winter boots," she said, returning. "I'm not going through the snow in flip-flops. Anyway, why should I? What for?"

(Though indeed, part of her was all in favour of going up the hill. If there is a way out, take it, take it! Don't stay here in this grisly hovel. If there is a path that goes on over the hill, you need not come back.)

"There's a pair of boots," said the creature on the bed. "Look again."

Impatiently, Sauna looked again, and there were boots; a pair that Aunt Floss had taken to a basement rummage sale two years ago because they were outgrown.

"These are much too small," Sauna said. "They don't fit any more."

"Cut the toes off, then, dearie."

"Look: what is it you *want*, up the hill? What's so important?"

"Book," said the creature. "Up the glen where the old monks used to live and sing. In days when I was young and pretty. Younger and prettier than *you*. Cave in cliff. Old Hermit's cave. Book, all wrapped up. You bring book."

The word *book*, three times repeated, echoed in Sauna's mind. In that queer snatch of overheard conversation, caught, goodness knows how, on the dead, disconnected television channel, Colonel Clipspeak had said, "They want to stir up more trouble," and Dakin—that's right—Dakin had said, "The book will help them."

Dear Dakin! To hear his voice had been like a sudden touch of warm sunshine on her face.

But the book. It was something important, then. Everybody wanted it. To make trouble?

"Why should I bring the book?" she said to the skeleton on the bed. "Who wants it?"

"Friends. My friends. When they come on King Edward's Day."

"Your friends."

"Astarte, Abiron, Asmodeus, Belial . . . Soon they come. In power and thunder. Bring the book for them, they give you power too."

"If they have that power," said Sauna, "why can't they get the book for themselves?"

"Human hands—human eyes."

Will they really come? Can she mean it? Sauna wondered. I hope I'm not here then. Let Aunt Floss entertain them on her own. The Princes of Air.

She had a sudden swift shuddering vision of someone with a blue crest on his head, like snow blown backwards in a gale, with bright, cold, curling flames under the soles of his feet, with flesh transparent as water, with seaweed floating among his bones . . .

If those are her friends, I don't want to meet them.

She tried on the boots.

They were certainly far too small.

By the time the crew of the *Cockatrice Belle* had cleared and mended a way for themselves across the flat watery plain of Clackmannan, dusk was falling. The formidable shadowy height of King's Seat Hill and Ben Cleuch rose up on their left like a black wall; no lights twinkled ahead where the towns of Tillicoultry and Dollar might be supposed to lie. The River Devon crept and wriggled like a pale glimmering serpent in the valley. The landscape was ominously quiet, as if something in it was gathering for a pounce.

"I don't like it," muttered Colonel Clipspeak to Major Scanty. "It ain't *natural* for a place to be so quiet. There ought at least to be rooks—or gulls or eagles flying about. Tell the men to keep on full monster-alert at all times."

"Certainly, Colonel. It will be too bad if the town of Dollar is entirely deserted. It used to be a pleasant little place when I spent time there as a lad."

"Oh, you know it, do you, Major?"

"I went to school there. McNab's Academy, you know."

The colonel did not know, and was not particularly interested, but said, "That is capital, then. Your familiarity with the town may stand us in good stead if there is a battle; which I greatly fear there will be. Ah, here is Dr. Wren. Do you not find this unusual quiet somewhat ominous, Archbishop? Deuced suspicious?"

The archbishop was in a high state of excitement. "Oh, yes, I expect they are mustering their forces," he said, "but listen to this, Colonel! I have solved the enigma of the paper, I have cracked its code. As I said, it is written in Ogham script."

"Ogham?"

"A mode of writing, using lines and crosses, employed by the ancient Irish. I daresay Michael Scott may have picked it up too, since he was a great linguist and polymath."

"Gracious me, Archbishop! So what does the paper say?"

"Oh, well, nothing much that we did not know already: the paper is a kind of testament; Michael Scott asks that his book be interred, not with him at Melrose Abbey, but in what he calls 'the sacred cave' at Sorrow Abbey—'so that profane, unhallowed fingers may not unearth and examine its hidden lore, whereby great and terrible mischief might ensue, but where it may rest safe and untouched until the Judgement Day uncovers all secrets'—"

"Does he say *where*, precisely, the sacred cave is to be found?" demanded the colonel impatiently.

"No, he says 'the locality of which is known only to the holy monks of Sorrow Abbey.' "

"Much use that is to us! Since they all died out several hundred years ago!" exclaimed the colonel. "But—wait a moment—you were saying, Major, that you were familiar with the environment of Dollar and Glen Sorrow?"

All along the train men were preparing for the battle, which everybody felt sure would take place very soon. The only uncertain factor was what particular kind of opponent would they be fighting? Trolls and Kelpies seemed probable in a region so close to the Firth of Forth. But then there were the Ochils to the north, so dark and menacing—who knew what unknown perils might lurk among their crags, covered now in snow?

Major Scanty, when consulted, had suggested the Chichevache, a kind of bony monster with horns; but fortunately this creature preferred a diet of females—which might explain the lack of them to be seen about the countryside, but made it less dangerous to the crew of the *Cockatrice Belle*. Two-horned Bycorns were also to be expected, and Chimeras, which had lions' heads, goats' bodies, and serpentine tails.

"No wings, luckily," said Scanty. "So they may be picked off by the same weapons that are in use for Kelpies. But I am

afraid the most likely enemy we have to expect will be Mirkindoles and Gorgons."

"Gorgons?" said Sergeant Bellswinger. "Then we must
issue all the troops with Snark goggles. Lucky we've been
recharging 'em as we came along. Gorgons are no joke."

"What do Gorgons do?" asked Corporal Nark.

"Lassy me, Nark, where have you been all this time? They
turn you to stone."

"That's nasty."

Private Minch, who was of a nervous disposition and
given to Seeing Things at moments of stress, here upset the
people around him by having a Seeing, and declaring that he
saw a small stone image of Bellswinger right above the
Sergeant's head.

"Oh, stow your gab, Minch," everybody said, and Private
Coldarm gave him an arrowroot jujube which he sucked in
tearful and hiccuping silence.

As well as polishing their weapons and Snark goggles,
most of the men got out lucky charms and gave them fond
and respectful attention.

Corporal Nark had a silver threepenny piece from a
Christmas pudding; Ensign-Driver Catchpole had a bit of
rock from Mount Vesuvius; Private Brag had a leaf from a
handkerchief tree on the island of Sark where his gran lived;
Sergeant Bellswinger, unexpectedly, now revealed his secret
parcel to be a square foot of turf from the centre of the Manchester United football ground.

"I just thought maybe it'd bring me luck," he explained
rather apologetically. "And nobody was using the pitch while
we were in Manchester; except Snarks, that is. So I just reckoned I'd help myself to a chunk. I think Flint must have seen
it in my cabin and he tried to half-inch it. Wouldn't have

done him any good, though. You have to take it for yourself. Well, it must be lucky, when you think what feet have trod it. O' course I'll be sure to return it once the state of emergency is over."

He had kept it watered by an ingenious system of guttering from the train roof. "Rain water, you see, that's what it's used to—" And now anybody who liked was allowed to touch it with a reverent finger.

As the train crept towards where the town of Dollar ought to be, facing across the valley floor towards Ben Cleuch and the twin glens of Sorrow and Care, with ruined Castle Campbell mounting watchful guard between them on its hillock, Dakin fell into a great state of worry and gloom.

Like the rest of the men he was tremendously keyed-up, positive that a great battle was impending, perhaps the decisive battle of the campaign. If they could win this one, might not the rest of the monsters take flight for good? That was what many of the crew believed. And then the train could turn southwards again, and they could all go home and start rebuilding their lives.

But Dakin felt miserably uncertain. He longed to be in the thick of the battle, beating his drum—but would he be allowed? Or was he still in total disgrace with the colonel? Would he be confined to the little hot room behind the engine, like a naughty child? He sought comfort with Uli in the galley, but Uli was in a queer state, nervous and whining; and Mrs. Churt was in bad skin, because the colonel had asked her to serve out an extra ration of turnip pancakes to all the men at their battle stations and so she was unusually busy and had no time for conversation.

As well as this, her great piece of cross-stitch, now completed, hung draped over the ironing-board in the galley.

Every single man on the train found time to come and touch it, at least once, before the battle. Some touched it half a dozen times, coming back repeatedly.

"A very interesting example of folk-lore in process of development," said Dr. Wren, who was helping Mrs. Churt with the pancakes. "Do they think it will bring them luck?"

"Well," said Mrs. Churt, "they seem to. It gives them a good feeling, like, and that'll help them to watch out and be extra nimble in the battle, I reckon."

Dr. Wren nodded, and touched the cross-stitch himself. So did the colonel, under pretext of making an official inspection.

"It's just airing now," Mrs. Churt told him. "We'll hang it over the piano when the battle's done."

To Dakin's great surprise, Major Scanty came in search of him.

"Ah, there you are, Dakin, my boy; just step along with me to the engine cabin, will you. Now, pay close attention," the major went on, when they were alone in the small room. "The colonel has an assignment for you tomorrow; during the battle, which, as you know, we expect will take place very shortly—"

"Oh, sir! Major! Do I get to play my drum?"

"No, my boy; the colonel wants you to go off in search of your cousin, under cover of the action—taking advantage, you see, of the general confusion—it will be an excellent opportunity for diversionary tactics, the colonel thinks. You must take the Gridelin hound with you, of course."

"Can I bring my drum along?" asked Dakin hopefully.

"No, my boy, that will not be necessary. In fact I should think it might be a decided encumbrance. Your cousin is very likely being held in some hiding-place in the mountains—up a steep and narrow track—"

Dakin's face fell, but he privately resolved that he *would* take his drum, just the same. After all, you never knew. Gorgons might react to it in the same way that Snarks did.

"I myself shall accompany you," Major Scanty disconcerted him by adding, "for I have a long acquaintance with the town of Dollar and its surroundings. I was a boy at school here and have often explored up Glen Sorrow to the ruins where the old monks used to have their monastery."

"Thank you, sir," said Dakin, politely but without marked enthusiasm.

"So you must now make yourself ready—and the hound too, of course—and then, the moment the alert sounds and the train stops, you and I will make a dash for it. Do you understand?"

"Yessir."

"Very well. I will meet you shortly near the observation platform."

These instructions from the major left Dakin in a mixed frame of mind, half satisfaction, half bitter disappointment. He had hoped so *much* to have this own important role in the battle again, as at Manchester; to feel part, and a very crucial part at that, of what was going on. Instead here he was, fobbed off with a rescue errand, sent in search of his cousin Sauna.

But still, Dakin had to acknowledge, there was a good deal of sense in it. He knew Sauna well—and he was the only one who could talk to the dog in German—and the dog was fond of him, and loved Sauna dearly, and would certainly be able to track her down if she was anywhere near at hand—yes, he supposed there was really no fault to be found with the plan, so far as practical sense went; and Sauna might very likely be in horrible danger with her Auntie Floss—if it were really Auntie Floss—and that greasy, creepy Tom Flint. Only—only he did so *wish* that he could be in the battle!

But there it was . . .

Dakin and Uli were soon stationed in the cabin next to the observation platform, looking out past Colonel Clipspeak's elbow. Dakin's drum was concealed by his Snark cape, and Sauna's skipping-rope was in his pocket. Uli was whining faintly with excitement.

"*Devilish* peculiar countryside round here," Clipspeak muttered to Dr. Wren. "I don't wonder its history is so full of witch-burnings and wizardry. It has a deuced spooky and unchancy feel to it, if you ask me! Something to do with those deep cracks between them mountains, coming right down to sea level. It ain't a bit surprising that whoever's organizing the monsters chose to have their mustering place up here—wonder where, though? In Dollar, do you think?"

"The town looks wholly quiet—uninhabited, one would say—" began the archbishop.

Just then all the train's alarm bells went off, as half the sky appeared to fall on them. Teeth, beaks, talons, iron claws, razor-sharp bronze pinions hissed through the air, huge wings flapped, flaming eyes darted rows of sparks like rocket fire.

"*Now!*" hissed Major Scanty to Dakin as the train jerked to an abrupt standstill. "Pay no heed to all that botheration— just you stick to my heels, you and the hound."

He dropped off the platform with the agility of a man half his age. Dakin followed, with Uli loping eagerly at his side.

So far as could be seen in the dusk, the train had not yet reached the main station of Dollar, but stood in a siding on the edge of town. Dakin and the major ran down the slope of an embankment and crossed a stretch of marshy meadow; very soon they were ascending a moderate uphill slope, with the ruined Castle Campbell sticking up like a broken fang above them on their right.

Uli, who had seemed startled and baffled for a moment

or two when they first left the train with all the noise of whistles and gunfire raging about them, now let out an eager whine and pulled ahead of Dakin, dropping his nose to the trail. "Here, boy, sniff this," said Dakin, and fetched out the skipping-rope. Uli gave a yelp of excitement.

"Aha!" exclaimed Major Scanty in triumph. "The dog has found the scent! This is the foot of Glen Sorrow—" He stopped and gasped suddenly, pressing a hand to his chest. Then he coughed, and coughed again.

"Agggh! Devil take it! Of all the cursed luck! I have been pierced, I fear, by a Telepod. Their tusks are detachable. One has gone right into my diaphragm."

"Oh, *sir!*" Dakin exclaimed in horror. "Won't you—what shall I—do you want me to pull it out?"

"No, my boy; if it were pulled out, I should bleed to death on the spot. My only chance is to try to make my way back to the train. Do you go on. The dog plainly thinks he knows the way."

"But, sir—"

"Don't stop, my boy, don't wait! I think time may be precious. If you should find me still here, on your way back, *then* will be the occasion—" The major coughed again and collapsed on the ground.

Gulping with fright and shock, Dakin ran on up the hill, his arms half pulled from their sockets by the impatient Uli, who had his ears up, nose down on the track, tail flying out behind him in the wind of his progress.

One thing, thought Dakin, at least the major didn't have time to tell me off because I'd brought my drum with me. Maybe he never noticed it. Poor old Major, I just hope he makes it back to the train.

*   *   *

With the close approach of King Edward's day, the Being who presented herself as Auntie Floss appeared to take on greater power. Her thin, hissing voice gained volume, she gabbled a great deal more. A large part of what she said was unintelligible to Sauna. Sometimes she addressed other people: Azrael, Abiron, Chezroth. Sometimes Sauna thought she heard voices replying, voices that echoed outside the cottage, that clanged like brass over the thatched roof, howled among the trees.

"They are getting ready," Auntie Floss said. "When you bring them the book—"

"I shall not bring any book," Sauna said. "Never."

"You had better think again about that. Go and look at the television."

Without wishing or meaning to do so, Sauna went. This tended to happen more and more. The set was not even switched on, but she saw an old lady on the screen who wailed and wept: "Arch, I didna dae whit they tell it me, an' syne they burned off my feet, look—" and the old woman exhibited two hideously charred stumps—"Ach, I hired wi' them, but I didna do whit they ordered and I'm for perdition juist the same. Be warned by me, lassie . . ." and shrieking she threw her shawl over her head. Sick and appalled, Sauna went back through the front room and opened the outside door. But the weather had worsened again, snow fell in thick strips, the gale howled.

"You know I can't go in this, it would be hopeless hunting for some old book," she said. Had the picture on the screen been just a trick to fool her? "Anyway, the boots don't fit. I outgrew them two years ago."

"Don't disobey me, child. Cut the toecaps off the boots and put them on."

"No!"

The figure half rose from the bed, yellow teeth bared in a savage grin. Sauna, who had prepared herself as best she could for some such confrontation, wrapped her hand in a rag, snatched the iron bar from the fire, and waved it defensively in front of her. To her horror, Aunt Florence gripped the bar at its red-hot end, twitched it from Sauna's grasp and tossed it out through the open door. The hand that had held the bar was black as burnt toast, but she appeared to feel no pain.

"You had better do as I tell you," the voice said.

Shocked to death Sauna crept away, found the only knife and began hacking at the toes of the boots. Well, if I can get them over my feet, I suppose I might still escape, she thought rather hopelessly.

Maukin, the grey rat, now ventured off the bed more often and made questing forays over the wrinkled newspapers on the floor. Just the sight of him turned Sauna queasy with terror and repulsion—the way he scuttled, with greasy speed, from one spot to another, keeping if possible in the angle of the wall, with his long scaly tail slithering behind him, his sharp red eyes fixed on Sauna. He had eaten her one remaining shoe; or, at least, she could not find it anywhere. Her muscles twitched with the impulse to deal him a bash with a three-legged stool, but she knew she would never catch him; he was infinitely too quick for her.

After she had sliced one toecap from a boot she left the cup-shaped bit of leather lying on the yellow newspaper. The rat scooted out from the wall, seized it and gnawed up the stiff semicircle in two chews and a swallow.

"He'd chew off your feet, if I told him," twittered Auntie Floss gaily and threateningly.

"You think I'd let him? I'd kick him from here to—"

"Ah, my suckling, but I could put you in a deep sleep. And then what? Just fancy . . ."

The frightening thing was that Sauna suspected this was true. If she let her eyes remain for too long on the hateful yellow grinning face (not that she ever intended to, goodness knew, but sometimes it seemed to happen by compulsion) she could feel herself becoming drowsy, slipping into a helpless, trancelike state in which this crazy, cut-off life in the cottage seemed like a bad dream, *was* only a bad dream, perhaps . . .

What terrified her was the idea that, lulled, mesmerized into such a state, she might do anything that Floss told her, go and fetch that book, cut off her own means of escape perhaps.

Gritting her teeth, Sauna somehow shoved her foot into the left boot—it was agony—and began carving at the right one. She felt hollow with hunger and weakness. They had almost come to the end of what was edible in the cardboard box. All that remained was dry mustard, paraffin wax, knife powder, and dandelion coffee.

"Would you like some dandelion coffee, Aunt Floss?"

One of Sauna's own weapons, kept up for her own satisfaction, was the pretence that she *believed* the thing on the bed was her aunt, had any connection with her family. Since coming to the cottage she did not believe so. Even in Manchester, Sauna thought, even in Spain when she came to fetch me, I don't reckon she was ever who she said she was. She was sent to get hold of me. But why? Just for that book? Why do they need it? And who are *they?*

Climbing up the track in a snowstorm, Dakin and Uli came to the point where a huge fir tree had fallen and blocked the way. Uli let out short angry barks of frustration, and ran back and forth as if undecided which way to go. Down below on their right was a cliff, dropping to a gorge. That was no use. They must climb up to the left then, thought Dakin, gazing in dismay at the huge mass of wreckage. And it was growing dark . . .

Then he remembered his Kelpie gun. What could singe and scare off a Kelpie might perhaps do useful work burning a way through all this debris of timber and branches and needles and twigs.

He tried it, and blasted a highly satisfactory alleyway in among the wreckage. Uli, on his haunches, watched with intelligent eyes and whined eagerly.

It worked well. But there was a very long way to burn through the wreckage. And I'm making a devil of a lot of noise and commotion and sparks, thought Dakin. This rescue job's supposed to be done quickly and quietly, while the battle's going on. Suppose the row fetches along some Chimeras or Basilisks? Still, there's nothing for it; I just hope the battery doesn't run out. On he went, burning, stamping and hacking.

Mercifully the battery lasted—almost to the end, at least. Dakin had to slash away the last few yards of wreckage with his Kelpie knife. And I hope to Habbakuk, he thought, that we don't come across another fallen tree. For if we do, we're done.

Uli bounded through and ran joyfully ahead as soon as the tree was passed; Dakin had to race to keep up with him.

But now just what Dakin had feared came to pass: a flock of winged attackers plunged down on him. It was too dark to make out what they were; but plainly their intentions were hostile.

His knife was blunted, his battery run down. What the pize am I supposed to do now?

Then the simple answer came to him: his drum.

He whisked off the cape, unshipped the drum from its portage sling, whipped out the drumsticks, feverishly screwed up and tightened the twitches, and beat out a wild noisy tattoo: titherum-tum-tum, titherrum, titherum, tum, tum, tum!

Rat-tat-tat, rattle-rattle-rattle-tat-tat.

The creatures above sheered off, dismayed and thwarted. They vanished into the black trees overhead.

But then a worse menace appeared: a far, far worse menace.

Wreathed in horrible grey luminosity it came towards him down the track—bigger than a grizzly bear, deadly, pitiless, unspeakably terrifying. A Mirkindole.

Now I really am done for, thought Dakin. No use beating my drum at *him*.

Mirkindoles are deaf, he remembered the archbishop once telling him. No use trying to frighten them off with noise.

And indeed it could be seen that Uli, who was half bursting himself with hysterical barks and snarls, made no impression at all on the creature. On it came, implacably.

It had a tiger's body: huge, sleek, muscular, rippling, striped; twice the size of any normal tiger. And, strangely, at the front of this formidable body was the face of an elderly, peevish man, framed between two massive curling horns. The face looked irritably at Dakin, as if he presented a disagreeable task, which it would be best to get over with as soon as possible. The Mirkindole paused, raised a paw the size of a tractor-wheel—in which could be seen a dozen curved claws each capable of ripping out someone's throat.

What had Dr. Wren said was the best way to deal with a Mirkindole? It's the same as—some other creature, same family. *Which? What* had he said?

The muscles of Dakin's mind seemed paralysed with terror. They refused to function.

Which other creature? Which?

Then the muscles of his mind finally released their grip and let go. With a gulp of relief he remembered. Basilisks, of course. You turn, the archbishop had said—he had a wound in his heel—you turn and look at them *over your shoulder*. Throw something. They detest bright colours.

Dakin dropped his weapons and plunged his hands into his pockets. What in the name of goodness was *this*?

He pulled it out, all the time envisaging that immense piece of live danger approaching him down the track, coming closer and closer—

The thing in his pocket was a little string sack of coloured candies; Pollylollies. How in the world could they have got there? He had not seen candies or sweets for ten years— longer. But it was precisely what was needed in the present crisis. He undid the string and flung handfuls of the little hard things over his shoulder at the advancing beast, staring into its gloomy face as he did so.

The Mirkindole paused, and brayed angrily: a sound that was more a bellow than a roar. It shook its head—one of the candies had evidently lodged in its eye. Staggering, it shook its head again; then lost balance completely and lurched over the edge of the track. Down it went, plunging and somersaulting, until it vanished from view among a clump of pines.

"Save us!" said Dakin. He drew a huge breath.

Uli, rather subdued, came and rubbed his head against Dakin's thigh. Then he shook himself, as much as to say, That's enough of *that*, and went loping on up the track.

Dakin, on legs that trembled a good deal, followed.

They reached a clearing. In the last of the daylight Dakin

could just see a little house; and that there was a dim glimmer at the window.

Outside the door Uli barked his head off. Dakin beat a terrific tattoo on his drum.

Uli did more than bark. He launched himself at the door like a battering-ram and burst it open. Without losing impetus, he hurled himself inside, and instantly Dakin heard a wild noise of battle; barks, snarls, growls, shrill, ugly screams, thuds, human cries, shrieks—

Dakin thundered on his drum as if possessed. He did not know why. He simply knew that he had to. This was why he had brought the drum all the way from London. It had nothing to do with battles. If I drum loudly enough, he thought, if I make enough noise, something crucial will happen. I have got to keep on. I have to. Thank heavens I brought it.

His wrists ached, his fingers were numb.

Out through the cottage door burst his cousin Sauna. She was thin, terribly thin, pale, and wild-eyed.

"Oh, Dakin!" she cried. Oh, Dakin! You're here! Oh, Dakin!

She caught hold of his arm and dragged him, still drumming, away from the cottage to the other end of the clearing, where the track made its entry.

Uli tore out of the cottage door after Sauna. He was still engaged in a fight, battling with something that was smaller but extremely savage, something that screamed and writhed and tore at the big hound. But finally he tossed his bleeding head in triumph and hurled away some heavy body that flew across the snowy space and thumped down out of sight.

"Uli!" cried Sauna. "Come here, come quick. Let's get away. Quickly, quickly!"

As they reached the edge of the clearing, Dakin had a view

of something standing in the cottage doorway outlined against flickering light, something so horrible that he quickly slammed his mind down like a shutter against the memory, and never in all his later life raised that shutter again.

Now there was a queer noise overhead. Voices? Thunder? More monsters?

"Keep going!" shouted Sauna in his ear. "Come on, Uli!"

Next moment an unbelievably loud roar further up the hill rose in volume until the sound was past anything that could be accepted by human ears—and a whole hillside of snow fell down from above on to the cottage, and then swept it hurtling down into the forest beneath the open space. And lower down the hill, out of sight. Not out of hearing though; they could follow its progress for many minutes crashing and booming its way into the valley far below.

"An avalanche!" breathed Sauna. "We got away just in time. Oh, Dakin!"

Speechlessly, they hugged one another.

Uli whined.

"Uli! *Meinhund! Liebhund!* Beautiful, beautiful dog!"

Sauna knelt down and hugged him too.

Then she cried out. "Oh, Dakin, he's hurt! Terribly hurt! He has a most awful wound in his neck. That rat—that foul rat—must have done it."

"Was *that* what it was? A rat?" Dakin said. "It must have been the biggest rat in the world." He shuddered, thinking of the other thing he had seen, the thing in the doorway. "Are you all right, Sauna? Are you sure?"

"Yes," she said hastily. "Yes, I'm all right. But we must get Uli back to the train—he's in a bad way."

Indeed, when the dog tried to stand, he staggered and fell down again.

"We'll have to carry him," said Dakin. "But how?"

Sauna frowned. Then she plunged a hand into her pocket and brought out a tangle of cord.

"I knew this would come in useful. We'll find two straight branches and lace the cord back and forth, to make a litter."

Although it was now dark, they could find what they needed easily enough in the snow. Dakin hacked a couple of branches with his Kelpie-knife. There was not quite enough cord, even with Sauna's skipping-rope, so Dakin undid the lacings of his drum and they made a kind of stretcher. Lifting Uli on to it was no easy job, for he was a massive weight and whined pitifully when they shifted him. But at last he was arranged with his weight well distributed and nothing important dangling over the side.

"It's going to be an awful job," said Dakin forebodingly.

"We're not leaving Uli behind," said Sauna. "She was going to set the rat on me. He came in just in time to save me."

It *was* an awful job getting Uli down Sorrow Glen. Sauna's feet were in agony from the too-tight boots. But at least the snow had frozen hard over the muddy stretch; and the fallen fir had been shaken from its perch by the thunder of the avalanche, and had slid further down the hillside, so they were able to get past it without difficulty.

"It was your drumming that started the avalanche," said Sauna. "Loosed a great canopy of snow that was dangling from a cliff up above. I'm glad the cottage is gone," she added in a trembling voice.

She said nothing about its occupant.

"I knew I had to bring my drum," said Dakin.

He was worrying about Major Scanty. What would they ever do, how would they ever manage, if they found the major still lying where he had fallen, pierced by the Telepod tusk? They could not possibly carry both him and Uli. But they could not leave Uli behind . . .

Also, Dakin doubted if he and Sauna could actually carry the major, even between them. He kept an anxious lookout for the spot where the major had fallen, which he had memorized with care at the time: there was a slanting rowan tree and a split rock with heather growing in the crack.

Fortunately the major was gone. They found a few drops of blood on the snow, but no body.

"I do hope that means the old boy's all right. I do hope he managed to struggle back."

To their huge relief the *Cockatrice Belle*, seen across the water-meadows a few minutes later, was a blaze of light and activity. Dakin had nursed another secret fear, that the battle might have gone badly for the *Belle* and her crew, but no; there was the colonel on the observation platform, there was Dr. Wren . . .

"Sir, *Sir!*" yelled Dakin. "I've brought back Sauna! Here she is!"

Half a dozen willing helpers immediately jumped down to relieve Dakin and Sauna from the burden of Uli, who, to Sauna's great joy, had faintly wagged his tail at sight of the brilliantly illuminated train.

But then he suddenly let out a long, rolling, terrible growl.

"Why, Uli, what's up? There's naught but friends here."

Uli growled again, and they heard a faint voice crying in the darkness: "Help! Help, for pity's sake!"

They were standing in swampy, tussocky ground, the marshy meadows that lay between Dollar and the steep-sloping Ochils to the north. Behind Dakin a muddy ditch or brook wriggled like a black crack across the plain. And from this crack a black hand extended in supplication.

"Oh, please help me! I can't lift myself! I am in such pain! Please, please, for the love of mercy, don't leave me here to drown. The tide is rising! And I can't move."

"*Oh, no! Not again!*" muttered Mollisk. "It can't be! Not that slimy, dripsy squint-eyed Flint? What does he take us for? Sir, Colonel, it's that feller we rescued twice afore. Don't you reckon there's summat downright fishy about the way he keeps turning up? He takes us for sapheads. Don't you think we should just leave him there to drown when the tide comes in?"

The colonel had bounded down from the observation platform and was heartily congratulating Dakin and Sauna on their safe return.

"Happy to see you, Dakin, my boy. Excellent work, excellent! And little Miss Sauna too! Everybody on this train will be as pleased as can be to have you safe back. Dr. Wren especially—"

But at the news that Tom Flint had reappeared he spun round.

"*What's* that you say, Mollisk? *Flint?* Great Scott, that man must have the impudence of the devil himself to show his face again. But no, we can't leave him to drown, richly as he deserves it. The archbishop will certainly wish to interrogate him. Hoist him out, Mollisk and Clinch. Fetch him along, but don't leave him for a *moment*, keep him under close guard—"

Tom Flint's piteous cries and moans, as he was carried (none too gently) on board made the dog Uli growl even louder, and Sauna, who had been rapturously hugging Mrs. Churt, started violently and began to shiver.

"That voice of his! He was one of the two in the carriage. Don't let him near me!"

"Don't you worry, lovey, Sergeant Mollisk'll have him

clapped in irons afore you can say parsley sauce. Now you lads come along and bring the dog to my nice warm galley—and you, too, dearie. You look as if you need a deal of feeding-up—ginger and treacle pudding!"

"Oh, thank you, darling Mrs. Churt, only not ginger! Any other! But you said *Sergeant* Mollisk—has he been promoted? Where's Sergeant Bellswinger?"

"*Oh, dearie!* He got gobbled up by one of those nasty Mirkindoles! He didn't turn round quick enough, Private Clinch said—"

"Oh, *no!*" Sauna burst into tears. "I was s-s-so *much* looking forward to telling him all that happened to me," she sobbed.

Dakin, at that moment, was hearing the same news from Colonel Clipspeak. He was within an inch of weeping too, and had to swallow several times and bite his lip. Never again to have a fist like a leg of mutton thump him between the shoulderblades! Never to hear that friendly roar address him as "You little article."

"Wh-what about Major Scanty, sir? And Lieutenant Up-fold?"

The colonel sighed. "I'm afraid Upfold got demolished by a Troll. But Major Scanty was, happily, rescued by Dr. Wren who—with great intrepidity—dashed out through the thick of the battle when he saw the major dragging himself towards the train; and then cleverly packed the tusk that had stabbed the major with ice, so as to prevent excessive bleeding when it was withdrawn. Scanty is doing well, I'm glad to say. But now we must put a few questions to that miserable Flint. Dr. Wren is already with him. You had best come too, my boy; you were with the party that first encountered him at Willoughby."

"What about Sauna, sir? Shall I fetch her?"

The colonel pondered.

"She may not be ready for a confrontation just yet; poor gal, she looks as if she has been through a bad time."

Flint had been carried to his former quarters, the small cabin behind the engine. Clinch and Tussick stood guard outside the door.

"Dr. Wren's in with the blighter at the moment," Tussick told the colonel in a low tone. "It's a mighty queer thing, sir—you'll hardly believe this, but it's a wonder the cove is alive at all. He's hardly any right to be. *Both his feet have been burned off at the ankles.*"

"What? Can you be serious, man?"

"True as I stand here, Colonel. Dr. Wren's bandaged the stumps with honey and cobwebs; he and Mrs. Churt say that's best for burns. Unusual sort of mishap, though, ain't it? We don't get many burns among our battle casualties."

Dr. Wren came out of the cabin. He looked grave. A wailing, pleading voice from inside the room sobbed. "Please bring her! Oh, please bring her here! And tell her to bring the doll as well! For pity's sake!"

"What the deuce is the fellow on about?" demanded the colonel. "Has he admitted that he was the one who abducted the gal? Or why he took her?"

"He has done so in a way. I'm afraid he is without doubt a lost soul." The archbishop looked rather sick. "He has told me a long, long rigmarole, beginning with the very first shameful bargain he made with the Evil One at the early age of seven—he did something he shouldn't, something disgusting, and then bought immunity from punishment, in exchange, you know, for the usual servitude, and so it has been all his life, ever since. Now, his only hope seems to be that Sauna can rescue him."

"Rescue him from *what?*" demanded the colonel.

Dr. Wren shrugged.

"The last, worst fate of all."

"But why should Sauna be able to? Why should she want to?"

"That would be for her to say," said Dr. Wren.

"Shall I fetch her?" offered Dakin.

"Only if she is entirely willing," the archbishop told him. "And, Dakin, he keeps talking about dolls. Tell her to bring the dolls, if she has them."

"What dolls? Oh, yes, I remember."

As Dakin ran away down the corridor he heard Dr. Wren say, "She is a good, courageous child. I think it likely that she will come."

In the galley Sauna said, "Dolls? But I only have one left. One got burned up. I fell asleep by the fire . . . and, when I woke . . . one of them was quite gone . . . and the other . . . I just managed to snatch it out—"

She plunged a hand into her pocket and exhibited the tiny singed mannikin in his black hat and blue cravat. "Poor little object—I doubt he's not worth mending."

"Well, bring him along; if you really don't mind coming, that is," Dakin told her. "Dr. Wren said, only if you are truly willing—"

"Now, don't you do a single thing you don't want to, dearie," said Mrs. Churt.

Sauna sighed.

"Oh, yes. I'll come. I feel better now. And I don't think *anything* could be as bad as what I've seen already."

Dakin felt, as he followed her along the corridor, that she seemed ten years older. He had a lot of catching up to do.

As soon as Tom Flint laid eyes on Sauna, he started to cry and hiccup.

He was lying on a narrow bunk, wrapped in white bandages from neck to knees. The bandages ended below his knees.

He wept and wailed and prayed, his mud-coloured eyes fixed all the time on Sauna.

"Oh, please! Oh, please! I'm in such pain! All over! Burning, blistering pain! You are the only, only one who can help me!"

The archbishop laid a kindly, supporting hand on Sauna's arm as she stepped into the confined space of the cabin. But she gently shook her head and moved forward.

"Why should I help you?" she asked the man in the bunk.

"You escaped, didn't you? You got away? I didn't take you—right—up to—to—the door. You had a chance to get away. Didn't you? And you took it. You did get away. Here you are, now!"

The eyes, like pools of slime, beseeched her.

Sauna said calmly, "You stopped where you did because a tree had fallen. You couldn't get by."

"Oh, please, oh, please. Don't hold that against me. Perhaps the tree was meant to fall. And you could do such a noble, noble deed. You could save me for ever."

"I rather doubt if that is the case," remarked the archbishop dispassionately.

Sauna looked with care into Tom Flint's bony, damp, beseeching face.

A thoughtful pause ensued. Then she said slowly, "Aren't you still hoping to catch me? Isn't this another try for a last-minute bargain with—with Somebody?"

"No!" screamed Flint, looking wildly round him. "No, no, no, no! I swear it! Never! I swear!"

"Swear by what name?" demanded the archbishop in a voice of iron. "By what authority?"

The man on the bed winced and writhed, as if he had been exposed to searing heat.

"Only help me!" he begged Sauna. "It can't do you any harm. And it will deliver me out of torment. Just give me the dolls." He kept his eyes away from Dr. Wren.

"But only one doll is left," said Sauna.

She drew it from her pocket—the small, soiled puppet in his black hat, white shirt, and blue cravat. The trousers were torn. The wooden feet were merely charred stumps.

Tom Flint's eyes lit amazingly at sight of it. They glowed. He made a restless movement. But his hands, Dakin saw, were manacled together.

"Free my hands, please, please! I can't run. I can't possibly escape. How could I?"

Wren and Clipspeak looked at one another.

"What do you think, Archbishop?" asked the colonel dubiously.

The archbishop rubbed his chin.

"I must say, it's hard to see what he could achieve."

"Undo the handcuffs, then, Clinch," ordered the colonel.

Clinch stepped smartly forward and did so. The hurt man on the bed rubbed his hands slowly together several times. The movement reminded Dakin of a snake he had once seen, rubbing off its shed winter skin.

He felt a sudden sense of alarm and mistrust. He leapt forward.

"Don't let him touch Sauna!"

The man on the bed had reared up, like a cobra about to strike, reaching for Sauna. Dakin pulled her back. She let go of the tiny doll, which fell into Flint's groping, grabbing hands. Instantly there was a blinding flash and a shatteringly loud crack of sound, as if from a chemical explosion. The cabin filled with thick, acrid, white smoke.

"Out of here! Quick!" yelled the colonel. "Get the gal out first."

They all tumbled into the corridor, coughing, gasping, and blinded.

"Fetch Snark masks," ordered the colonel.

But by the time the masks were fetched from the quartermaster's store there was no need to put them on. The sour, choking fumes had cleared as rapidly as they came.

From inside the cabin there was no sound at all.

"Mollisk," said the colonel, after a few moments, "put your mask back on, go in there with your ray-pistol cocked, and see what's up."

"Yessir."

Mollisk went in and came back round-eyed, pulling off his mask.

"Sir, Colonel, you'll never believe this—"

"Well, what?" snapped the colonel.

"He ain't there! Only a big lump of summat—"

Impatiently, the colonel pushed Mollisk aside and went in to the cabin himself, closely followed by Dr. Wren, Dakin, and Sauna.

Mollisk was perfectly correct. On the bed lay a large, brownish, greyish, whitish lump of substance, roughly the size and shape of a man.

Dr. Wren tapped this cautiously with the earpiece of his spectacles.

"Stone," he said quietly. "The man has turned to stone. In fact, to be quite precise, he has turned into a piece of Flint. I think this must be regarded as a diabolical joke. We are left with the substitute. The real essence of the man has gone—who knows where? But, I think we are safe in concluding, nowhere *at all* comfortable."

"Your doll has gone too," Dakin said to Sauna.

"I wouldn't have wanted it, not ever again." Then, turning to Dr. Wren, Sauna said, "Do you know, sir, I once stole that doll?"

"You did my child?" He did not seem in the least surprised.

"Yes! From Woolworth's! When I was six. And my mam was so angry with me, when I came home with it, that she made me go back and tell the lady at the counter what I had done. And, do you know, the lady, *she* wasn't angry—not exactly—but she paid for the doll herself, and the other one as well, and gave them to me. She said having them would remind me never in my whole life to take a thing that wasn't mine."

"You were luckier than Tom Flint," said the archbishop sadly.

"But, sir," Sauna said to the archbishop later, when they happened to be alone together.

"Yes, my child?"

"What has all this been *about?* Who was Auntie Floss, *really?* And Tom Flint? Why did he snatch me? And who was with him? And what did they have to do with the monsters? And what was the book that Auntie Floss kept nagging at me to go and fetch? Why couldn't *she* get it—if she could get all the way from Manchester to Scotland? And what was that awful voice—the one that said 'unloose the tempest,' the one Tom Flint called Master? Who was *He?*"

Sauna's voice wobbled a little; some memories were still hard to face.

Dr. Wren considered. He said, "You know that always,

from the very beginnings of life as we know it, there has been a continual, non-stop conflict between good and evil—the forces that we call good and evil?"

"Has there?" asked Sauna doubtfully.

"Of course there has! The whole universe is balanced between pairs of opposites—good and evil, night and day, up and down, winter and summer. And, on the whole, the state of equilibrium is maintained. But every now and then one side weighs heavier than the other. Things begin to tilt. More often in the direction of *down*, of darkness. Chaos encroaches. It is what we call the Sleep of Reason; society begins to crumble—"

"Wait, sir, wait! Stop! What's the Sleep of Reason?"

"It is what happens when the level of wickedness in several people's minds begins to combine together and forms a force that can, temporarily at least, overcome the forces of honour and good sense and law. What—for instance—caused the hole in the ozone layer? It was greed and stupidity, a rush to make profits before the dangers of new industrial processes had been thoroughly explored. So, what resulted? Monsters found their way in."

"But—but,—but someone *sent* the monsters—who did that? Why?"

"It was the total sum of all that greed and wickedness in people's minds. We give it a name. We call it Satan, the Prince of Dark. Human beings who surrender totally to this force may become temporarily endowed with *super*human attributes—but only temporarily. Like Mrs. Monsoon, like Tom Flint. It is borrowed power, soon spent."

"Why did they want that book? Why did they want *me* to fetch it?"

"Every few generations," said Dr. Wren, "there will be born a human intelligence far in advance of his time. Plato,

Galileo, Leonardo. Of this kind was Michael Scott. It is thought he anticipated Einstein, that he had discovered nuclear physics, a parallel universe—and, also, terrible ways in which one human group might wreak havoc on another. Such a book, in the wrong hands, might lead to unutterable devastation. His secrets are safer forgotten, until human society has progressed far enough to be able to use them unselfishly, for the good of the whole universe."

"But," said Sauna, still thinking of Aunt Floss, "why couldn't they get the book themselves? If they had all that power?"

"There had to be a human instrument who could understand and serve this purpose. You were the choice of the higher powers—the dark angels—perhaps because you were Michael Scott's descendant. And may have mental abilities of which you are still unaware. Aunt Floss was too old and crazy, Flint too untrustworthy. They were soon discarded. But you were young, with unknown potential."

Sauna found that she did not wish to think about this suggestion. She said, "Will there always be good and evil, sir?"

"So far as we can hypothesize. But they may be on different levels—ones that we can only guess at."

Sauna shivered. The prospect of this eternal struggle was daunting and tiring. Uli laid his head on her knee and sighed deeply, and she rubbed his bristly brows.

Dr. Wren looked at her with sympathy. She had, he thought, probably a long, unguessed-at course ahead of her, a hard way, very likely a dangerous one.

"But your Cousin Dakin will help you," he murmured, half to himself.

"When is King Edward's Day?" Sauna enquired, after a moment or two.

"It is today. On it there is a powerful conjunction of occult planetary forces, when our opponents should have reached their highest peak of strength. From now on their power will dwindle; I think we can hope for a period of peace and quiet." He smiled. "Until they are ready to make another attack. But by that time we, you and I, may well be in our graves, somebody else will have the job of fighting them off."

"Well, thank goodness for that," said Sauna, yawning. "Who was King Edward?"

"An obscure Scandinavian monarch with a talent for astronomy . . ."

But Sauna had fallen asleep with her head resting on Uli's shaggy brow.

Colonel Clipspeak said to Dakin, "My boy, you did well. Very well. And I am bound to say that Sergeant Bellswinger always spoke highly of your work. I am going to promote you to ensign, with automatic advance to sub-lieutenant at the end of eighteen months."

"Can I go on playing my drum, sir?"

"Harr—um. Sub-Lieutenants do not usually play drums—"

"I wouldn't want to leave off doing that, sir."

"Well—well—if we are stationed in London you may go to regimental music school. Now, can you send Miss Sauna to me?"

"She's asleep, sir."

"Well—when she wakes."

When the monstrous lump that had been Tom Flint was hoisted up—it had to be done with heavy lifting tackle—the shape flew apart into an uncountable number of lumps no

bigger than pieces of fudge. These were all shovelled off the train and dumped along the rail-track.

"Just what was needed for the repair of the permanent way," said Ensign Pomfret cheerfully.

When the next day dawned it could be seen that the landscape around Dollar was littered with wreckage and thousands of dead monsters.

"Oh, why do there have to be battles?" sighed Sauna, making her way to the colonel's cabin. She had slept for fourteen hours, after having been carried to her bunk by Dakin and Mrs. Churt.

The colonel said to her, "My dear Miss Sauna, now that you have had a good night's sleep, and are feeling, I hope, rather more the thing, I would be much obliged if you could raise a radio connection with London; without you we found it almost impossible to do so."

"Of course, sir. Right away."

It was plain that the air waves were still much disturbed after the battle. But at her fifth try Sauna managed to make contact with Leicester Square. Dakin, beside her, carefully held the colonel's dress sabre propped up at an angle of thirty-eight degrees.

"Gladiolus, Gladiolus: are you there, Leicester Square? We appear to have won a decisive victory at Dollar and—so far as can be ascertained—subdued the northern monsters."

"Delighted to hear it," said Leicester Square. "But, Lord Ealing wants to know, what about the book? Michael Scott's treatise? Has it been located yet? Over."

"No, it has not been found. Our experts, Dr. Wren and Major Scanty, are here to tell you that it has almost certainly been destroyed in an avalanche. The cave where it was lodged has been swept down the side of Ben Cleuch into the Burn of Sorrow. I will give you map references." The colonel did

so. "No agency, either human or diabolical, can possibly re-
cover the book now. It has been destroyed. Or such is the
opinion of Dr. Wren and Major Scanty. And, it seems also,
of the Principalities and Powers of Dark who have been
ranged against us, for they all seem to have packed up and
left. Most of the monsters have been destroyed, and no new
ones are arriving. Over."

"Then why are you loitering about in Dollar?" asked
Leicester Square peevishly. "Pray make all possible speed
back to London. There is still plenty of clearing-up work to
be done in the south. Over."

"We have to stop in Manchester, sir, on the way. Over."

"Whatever for?"

"To—er—to replace a square of turf in the centre of the
football pitch. Over and out," said Colonel Clipspeak, looking fondly at Mrs. Churt's completed cross-stitch, which
hung in majestic folds over his grand piano.